MW00423915

Cover art by Howard Lyon

Chapter 1

The Vovokan transport ship was only a little larger than the *Iridar* had been. The mobile sand had been removed and replaced with a rubberized decking more suitable for Terrans. The interfaces all understood Terran links and provided the services they needed to operate in deep space. Though tiny compared to the *Clacker*, the *New Iridar* was faster, better armed, and stealthier than the original ex-UED scoutship that had taken Telisa to Thespera. Once again Telisa lived in a quarters the size of a large closet. It had no shower tube; everyone on board had to share the single shower that had been installed where the sand cleaner had been.

What difference does it make? It just serves to remind me even more of the fact I'm a slave now.

Telisa thought of her golden master for the thousandth time. Shiny had been a powerful ally. Now he was a cold and distant overlord. Without him to rely on, the mission ahead could be hard. She thought of the PIT team's watchdog, a Vovokan battle sphere the size of a small car sitting within their cargo hold. At the moment it was content to wait there and ensure they went to the assigned world. Telisa assumed it would emerge to monitor their progress once they had arrived.

I have to get the pieces of the team back together again.

Shiny had brought her Caden, Cilreth, Siobhan, Imanol and Jason. The alien told her Cilreth2 and Maxsym had died in the *Clacker* when its shields gave way under a salvo sent by Shiny's other ships. Their advanced, luxurious ship was gone. Not a single member of PIT had protested when Shiny told them they were staying on the team. Perhaps they were all glad to go back out to the frontier, far away from Shiny's new empire. For some, like

Caden and Telisa, there was also the shame of being considered an enemy of mankind.

Telisa walked out of her tiny quarters and headed for the galley's lounge.

Imanol's tough enough to go on. Cilreth, too. Caden took it the worst but he has Siobhan. Jason may be broken. He no longer worships us. But that could be a good thing.

Telisa arrived and met everyone at lunch time. Caden and Siobhan sat together on a black piece of convertiture currently shaped like a couch. His arm was thrown over her shoulders. Imanol sat alone, brooding as if angry, but Telisa recognized it as his neutral state. Cilreth stood behind a counter looking over their food. Telisa could tell her computer specialist had already taken a morning dose of twitch. Jason stood on the other side of the room. He watched Telisa carefully.

Cilreth took note of her arrival.

"We've been talking it over, Telisa," Cilreth said. "We all think we should hang tough with Shiny. If we all refuse to go without Magnus, he'll have no choice but to let him out of the Trilisk column to join us."

Telisa looked at them. She could see the whole crew in a wider spectrum than before, thanks to her new eye. She flicked through infrared and ultraviolet views by habit as she processed Cilreth's speech. Everyone looked back at her expectantly.

"That means a lot to me," Telisa said. "But I've been through this already. You see, Shiny has control of the entire Sol system. He can send teams to every planet he knows about without even sending us. He sent other teams when we came to Earth to oust the Trilisks. We're just one possibility to him. He knows us, which is good, and he knows we have experience. He also knows if he gives us Magnus, he might lose his hold over us."

"There's no guarantee he'll ever release Magnus," Caden said. Siobhan leaned into him a bit harder. The pair had been inseparable recently.

"What are you going to do in the long run? Really work ten years and hope?" Imanol asked.

"That depends. Do watchdogs only watch their warehouse or do they listen too?" Telisa asked.

Cilreth processed that odd question, then she shook her head.

"I don't think we're being listened to through the ship's internal sensors," Cilreth said. "But the bottom line is, I can't be sure. The battle sphere probably has a mass sensor like Shiny, and it may be sensitive enough to see our mouths moving and tell it what we're saying. Speaking aloud is probably less dangerous than sharing secrets over the links."

Yes. Shiny has proved beyond devilish when it comes to network infiltration and obfuscation. I'm sure that was raised to a high art on Vovok.

"I'm going to find more artifacts and get something to bargain with," Telisa said out loud. She let the edge of anger into her voice. *Or something to threaten him with,* she thought. The tone of her voice made her hostile intent known to the others.

"Just let us know how to help," Caden said.

Telisa was glad Caden had decided to remain on the team. She knew he excelled at so many skills she needed. He had taken the betrayal hard. He had gone from a promising UNSF recruit to a traitor in the fiasco of their revolution.

"Keep training. Get Jason up to speed. We're going to be a notch more cautious this time because we have less backup. We'll scan the target planet for a few days, re-create the environ for virtual training, and gather more clues before we set foot on the ground. We'll bring back enough to keep Shiny happy while we search for anything that can get us leverage."

"Do we have any robots?" asked Imanol.

Telisa shook her head. "Not really. Not like before. I have five of the old scouts. We have over two dozen attendant spheres. As far as real automated firepower, it's only the *New Iridar* and our watchdog. Of course we still have our rifles, pistols, swords, knives, and a case of glue grenades."

"I have a case of real grenades too," Imanol added.

"Why do old people always think glue grenades aren't real grenades?" Jason asked.

Imanol rolled his eyes. "It wasn't always just stunners and shockers and nets and glue, Mr. Salesman," Imanol said. "Things were more serious before you core worlders all went soft, and still are—"

"Out on the frontier," Caden finished for him.

Telisa remembered her special alien weapon. It was lost, but she still had the cloaking sphere and her breaker claw.

"Where are we going?" asked Imanol.

"I'm in the dark about most of it," Telisa said. "We're going to a place known by Vovokans, ruins of a race other than the Trilisks. I know it's a planet, not a space habitat. Our mission is a lot like what we've done in the past: investigate and pick up some alien technology to study and learn about."

"Then hand it over to Shiny," Imanol said. The resentment in his voice expressed his thoughts more honestly than his words.

"Let's see what we find, first, and what use we can make of it," Telisa said. The group ate lunch. Telisa took more than her share of food. Her amped body screamed for more calories. She could survive on the amount they ate, but that would curtail her energy. She saw Caden and Siobhan staring.

I'm going to have to tell them I'm Telisa3 soon.

Telisa decided she did not feel like telling them yet. She left to think it over.

For now, they might think I'm catching up on calories from when I was paralyzed by Magnus's absence.

She went to the cargo bay and set up a tool table as a workspace. She found it inadequate compared to her old lab on the *Clacker*. Not the least of its problems was the presence of a large battle sphere sitting a few meters away. Amorphous green light played lazily across its black surface, though Telisa did not know what the display meant. She did not talk to it.

Telisa sighed. She decided to take care of some other necessary business she had been putting off.

"Do you have time?" Telisa asked through her link.

"Yes. Let's do it," Cilreth sent back. Telisa left the watchdog alone with its thoughts.

She met Cilreth in a chamber set up as a sick bay for the transport ship. Cilreth brought her over to a padded medical table. On a small tray, two thin gray wafers sat inside clear sterile packs.

"You checked these things out?"

"Eight ways from extinction," Cilreth said. "Still... I can only be so sure."

Telisa nodded.

Jason had obtained upgraded links for Telisa and Cilreth before leaving Earth. Telisa's link had become dated while she was in hiding on the frontier. Also, her new eye streamed in much more detailed visual scans than her natural one, so it would be nice to have more optical bandwidth and storage. Her new link had orders of magnitude more storage than her own brain. But Telisa's main motivation was to remove her current link in case Shiny or the Space Force had tampered with it.

Jason's not a traitor, but if he was found by Core World Security...

If they knew he had links and they had tampered with them, she would be back to square one.

I guess I'd rather be monitored by CWS than Shiny. For now.

Telisa lay down on the table and deactivated her link. A hole opened in the table below her head. A small robot unfolded from under the table and started to examine her head with three scanner arms. Telisa knew the sensors and effectors in her brain would remain behind. It was only the central module she wanted to replace. It was a simple, common procedure. Telisa had had an upgrade swap done two times before. She realized she was not at all nervous.

I was scared last time I did this. Things have changed. This is a vacation compared to what I've seen.

The robot immobilized her head, zapped her local nerves, and drilled into the back of her skull. Telisa waited. It seemed to take longer than she remembered.

"Hang on. It's almost done," Cilreth said.

Some snag?

The robot kept working. A minute later, the link had been extracted. Cilreth fed in the new link. The robot plugged the tiny wafer back into Telisa's head. A bonder sealed the hole in her skull close to its original strength for gradual replacement with natural bone matter. She would have a scab on her scalp and nothing more.

"How's it looking?" Cilreth asked.

Telisa checked her services list and brought up a few of her internal monitors. She shuffled a picture of Siobhan and Caden from her artificial eye's memory to her link.

"Basic sanity check is working out," Telisa said.

"Ready to sync?" Cilreth asked. She spoke of Telisa's old link. All its private information remained to be moved to her new link.

"I'm going to sleep on it," Telisa said. "I can sync later."

Cilreth shook her head. "Brave words, woman. I wouldn't be able to live without my data for ten minutes."

"It could mean a lot," Telisa said. "There's some danger in it."

Cilreth shrugged. "If my stuff can't detect any spy software there, then it may be hopeless. If it's that advanced, it may end up on your new link anyway. With Shiny, it could even be a tiny hardware bug he put in your head."

"Maybe," Telisa said. Her tone said she was not buying it yet. "Keep the old one isolated. Don't worry. I don't expect the same from you."

"It would cripple me for weeks," Cilreth said. "I have a lot of my own software in here. Whole suites of crap you couldn't imagine."

"I believe you. And I meant it. Go ahead and sync yourself when you're ready. Speaking of which, it's your turn."

They switched spots on the medical table. Telisa accessed the instructions from the table. Of course, the procedure was mostly automated. She skimmed some dire looking emergency instructions.

If something goes wrong, I'll be left with a mess on my hands.

She checked for the presence of a full medical suite. It was there. Apparently the Vovokan ship had been well equipped. She allowed the robot to proceed.

It went even faster than her switch out had gone. Cilreth was up within a minute. They stared at their old links, coated in fluid, sitting on a tray.

Telisa decided to try out another of the reasons she had decided to upgrade. One of her link's internal services included a new emotion management suite. The link could suppress or enhance activity in parts of the brain related to emotions. She saw a concentration suite that could control emotion to improve focus on complex mental tasks. It was limited to one three hour cycle every twenty four hours.

I need to forget about Magnus for longer than three hours at a time.

"Can you remove the emotion management limitations?" Telisa asked.

Cilreth stopped working and looked at Telisa.

"Is that what this is about?"

"No, it's about anything Shiny may have done to the other link," Telisa said.

"I won't tamper with it. I've seen the research. If you leave those things on too long, you'll become a different person."

"I need to focus on this mission. I have to get Magnus back. The way I see it, suppressing my feelings both keeps me from despair and also will help me fix the problem."

"If you were able to do that, then you'd find that when you get him back, you wouldn't have any feelings for him anymore," Cilreth said. "In fact, after a week or two without emotions, humans don't tend to turn them back on again. And when you do, they take a long time to come back. If you turned it on for ten years, not only would you not care about Magnus anymore, you probably wouldn't even have a will to live. Three hours a day should be sufficient."

Telisa sighed.

"How about an endocrine pack?"

Space force soldiers had implants in the abdomen that could interact with their endocrine system by releasing compounds controlled through their link. The ability to change various bodily signals was sometimes useful in combat situations, as well as in dealing with the stress of prolonged engagements.

"You don't need one. You're young and healthy and... well, besides, you're Trilisk Special Forces now anyway. You've got way more advanced features built right in."

"Trilisk Special Forces. Nice one."

"Well, you know... Imanol and his pet names. He came up with it for Cilreth2."

Telisa nodded. "How did you know I'm not original?"

"I set up *New Iridar* with some basic Trilisk detection and warning systems. I noticed right away you're in a host body. Besides, the damn robot almost couldn't bore through your skull. It's harder than steel."

"We're not headed to a Trilisk world. So says Shiny."

"But the Trilisks visited other races and... well, spied on them, or ruled them, or something."

"I guess we have no choice but to risk it for Shiny," Telisa said.

"I know. Why aren't you the original?"

"I can do a better job like this."

"Then that goes for the rest of us, too," Cilreth said softly. Telisa did not pick up any hostility in Cilreth's mood, only curiosity.

She handled losing Cilreth2 better than I handled losing Magnus.

"Yes. Ask Shiny. I think he studies us and thinks of us as primitive animals. He wants to solidify my position as leader. Probably because I'm the one he has the most leverage over."

"Ah. So as the strongest and fastest of us, instinctually we'll fall into line behind you."

"Sorry," Telisa said. "But I think that's how Shiny thinks of us."

Cilreth nodded.

"Your priority has to be our security, as usual," Telisa said. "When the time comes..."

"Got it. And you?"

"I'm going to start a mini project to recharge my cloaker and the breaker claw. I should have what I need to accomplish it."

"Good luck. Don't blow yourself up."

"On a ship this small? It would probably blow us all up," Telisa said and walked out.

Chapter 2

Caden caught himself thinking about the action on the orbital command center of the UNSF yet again. He kept slipping off to relive the events in his imagination over and over. It was agony. He had betrayed the very organization he had spent years of his life preparing to serve.

Siobhan came through the tiny door of his quarters and flopped down with him in his sleep web. She smiled. He was glad her mission had gone so much better than his. Caden had shared his dismay with her a couple of times, but he had hidden the fact he could not let go of it. While she was around, he tried to focus on her success. Siobhan needed to find a new passion now that her revenge had been enacted.

She succeeded at her life's mission.

"It's that time," he observed.

"That's why I'm here! You pick first," she said. "Hi grav or low grav."

"No way. With you, that's a loaded question."

"I won't hold it against you."

"Prove it. Hi grav planet. Day or night?"

"Night," she said, slipping in closer and kissing him. He kissed her back, then broke away.

"Okay, time to train."

"Got it," she said, though her voice held disappointment.

"It's the only thing we can do to prevent it from happening to us."

It's the only thing we can do to keep from ending up like Telisa and Magnus. One of us dead. Or supposed to be dead.

She knew what he meant. "I know, Caden. I'm ready."

The training scenario generator was ready to give them a session. Caden activated it, then flipped his link over into VR mode.

The universe flickered out and reopened in another place created by the TSG. Thick jungle plants surrounded them, rods of green pointing straight upwards. The entire scene was in twilight. Caden immediately felt his feet settle into a mossy mixture of dead plant material and dirt. His limbs were heavy. The air was moist.

"I thought it was a night setup," Siobhan said over her link.

"It is what it is," Caden said. He knew sometimes their parameters could be changed as a way of keeping them on their toes. Telisa insisted on leaving an element of the unknown in most of their training. He looked up. The light source was a huge moon hanging in the sky. He pointed at it. Siobhan nodded.

They stood quietly for a moment, weapons in hand. Their links received mission information. Caden absorbed the mission summary:

Survive 20 minutes until help arrives. Stay together and be above the jungle canopy by the end for aerial extraction.

Caden checked his visual feeds. Two attendants floated through the twilight jungle within fifteen meters of their position. The plants were green, resembling Terran ferns, though they grew straight up. Caden pushed one experimentally with his boot. It was a stiff green rod, rising in defiance of the high gravity. The fern rod leaned, then fell over. It took down two other plants when it fell in a chain reaction.

"These plants are crazy. They fall like dominos," he said.

"But look at that. When they fall near the base of another one, it braces itself with the fallen ones." Caden looked. Siobhan had found a standing plant that had fused itself right onto other plant stems.

One of the attendants reported a disturbance. It picked up mechanical noise coming through the trees. Then one of the attendants dropped off. The other reported laser fire.

"Withdraw," Caden said. He moved away from the oncoming sounds. He glanced behind him. Siobhan dropped a sphere and followed.

"I left them a surprise," she said.

Caden transmitted a nonverbal acknowledgement code through his link.

The plants were so stiff they slowed him down. Though he could topple them, each one remained an obstacle as it collapsed. Caden started to dodge them. When he grazed one, the tiny branches popped off with a sound like breaking glass. The sound made Caden think they might be sharp like glass, too, so he told his Veer suit to glove up his hands.

They ran through the jungle. Caden dodged, jumped, and ducked continuously through the tough high gravity plants. He slipped around an especially thick trunk, then leaped over a pool of deep green muck. Caden came up on something he could not identify and slowed.

A fat, many-legged creature rotated in surprise at their arrival. It was smaller than Caden and covered in mud. The thing shot a stream of liquid at them. Caden hoped it was water. Caden's weapon came into line but he did not shoot. The squat, hippo-pig creature did not look dangerous.

Kaboom!

The first detonation sounded behind them. The initial sharp blast dampened down to a sound like a cathedral shattering as hundreds of the glassy plants broke. The grenade's detonation message reported: one mechanical, ninety five percent kill confidence. Caden looked at the largest trees nearby. Their trunks were massive, the size of a house, though they did not rise as far as those on Earth.

13

The creature flattened its bulk toward the ground. In its new position it looked like a pile of mud. Caden supposed it had been shocked by the noise of the explosion. They passed it and left it behind.

"We'll choose one and start to climb at the last minute," he suggested.

"I can't see far. That would be relying on luck."

"Yes."

"This one is nice and tall, looks easy to climb. Maybe we can circle back?"

"Good idea," he sent.

But more complicated. Still, I think I can time it since we know when we need to be ready for the pickup. Although the TSG may well cause that to go wrong and see how we handle it.

They ran around the candidate tree, heading away and using it for cover. Caden's legs felt heavy. His muscles burned. The heavy lateral movement was as bad as his increased weight.

Siobhan must be hurting big time. No matter how much she trains, she's built for lower gravity than Earth, and the simulation knows it.

Kaboom!

"That was my last one," Siobhan said between gasps of air. Caden slowed. He slipped a grenade out of his pack and held it back to her.

"Got it! Go! Go!" she urged over the link, though he saw her body wobbling.

Their other attendant went offline. He felt blind on the battlefield. The only thing Caden knew was there had to be more attackers out there. As they moved through the forest, Caden thought about their pickup. The trees looked easy to climb, though the gravity would make it more difficult.

"The trees are massive. They could take a grenade. We can save the last grenade for the base of the tree," he said.

"Okay," Siobhan transmitted. "As long as we're not in direct line of sight with the grenade. Some of these stiff shards will fly like knives." She would not have been able to say it out loud, Caden thought, because he could hear her gasping for air. It was nice to be able to talk through their links so they could concentrate on breathing rapidly.

Caden led them around in a large circle toward their right. He hoped the enemy was not numerous and advancing across a broad front. If they were, the circle back tactic could prove disastrous.

Fzzzzzzt.

Leaves ignited around them.

"They're faster than us!" Siobhan said. "I'm heating up!"

"Behind this tree!" Caden said. They were at another huge tree. Caden zig zagged around three glass ferns to the side of the trunk, then clambered around it.

"We can't make any distance," Siobhan said. Her face showed pain, though Caden could not tell if she had been burned. He accessed her Veer suit interface with his link. The suit reported it had almost absorbed its limit of energy in the rear torso panel. Another laser strike there would destroy the back of the suit and cook her alive.

"Your suit is overloaded. Run on ahead. I'll delay them here."

"Or I could turn to face them on the fresh side," Siobhan said, but they both knew the whole suit also had a shared energy reservoir that could only take so much. Part of the suit's defense was simple physical armor, and part of it was a webwork that could transfer and absorb electromagnetic energy.

"Go," he said.

Siobhan staggered on as Caden hugged the tree. He brought up his weapon. It was set for a mechanical target profile. He drew his spare laser pistol and armed it, too.

Some chance they'll come around the other side of the tree.

Caden tucked himself next to a ridge in the tree leading down to a large root. It gave him some cover from the back side just in case. Movement against his side caused him to start. The skin of the tree moved.

"The trees move," Caden blurted. He stayed calm. If the tree ate things that nestled among its roots, he was probably already toast.

"What?"

A machine ran out in front of him. It looked like a typical light combat machine: vaguely man shaped, metallic skin, holding a weapon usable by human soldiers.

Caden launched two rounds with his main weapon. He gave it a shot from his laser pistol as well. The machine went down in a burst of smoke.

"I'm okay," Caden clarified. "Just FYI the trees can move. Slowly. Or at least their skin undulates."

"Uh, great. Are we going to be able to climb it?"

"We'll make it. Smart ropes can do most of the work, if it comes to that."

Caden ran ten paces away from the tree after Siobhan and dove behind a log. He watched from a quarter meter of open space beneath it. Another machine ran out, making good time. It opened fire at the same time as Caden. Some unseen force ripped the laser pistol from his hand. Caden finished shooting his other weapon. His hand felt numb. Blood splattered across a nearby green plant like a bizarre decoration. Caden did not even bother counting his remaining fingers, he just turned and ran to find Siobhan.

"I hear fire," she transmitted from up ahead.

"I got two, I think. Running for you as fast as I can," he sent.

"Okay, I'm heading back around. I know the tree," Siobhan said.

Caden found her in the forest. He tried to move quickly and silently, but it was impossible.

It doesn't matter. The machines can hear us easily even if we were quiet.

Caden fell in behind Siobhan. She slowed to take a position beside him for a moment. He could hear her ragged breathing.

"Give me the last grenade. I'll buy you some time," she said.

"No, stick with me!"

"It'll take some time for the smart rope to crawl up. You can get started, then I'll just rush right up."

"In high gravity? Sucking wind like that?"

"The rope can help," she said.

Caden checked his link map. They still had fifty meters to go. He turned and fired ten rounds into the forest blind. Given their target settings for mech, he might get lucky, or at least cause the pursuers to pause just before the PIT members arrived at the tree. It was a desperate measure. Mechanical combatants might be set for fearless aggression or they might hang back to preserve themselves.

Their course brought them back to the tree they had decided on for extraction. No fire came at their heels. Caden brought out a smart rope and sent it climbing. It slid up like a snake, weaving back and forth against the ridged surface. The gray skin of the tree moved in response, but it did not impede the progress of the rope.

Here's hoping we're nothing more than a brief irritation to a harmless life form.

They leaped up and started to climb. As soon as Caden made it to the first branching, he checked on Siobhan's progress in the heavy gravity.

Instead of following him, Siobhan shuffled back down the rope.

"Their lasers can still kill us up here," she said. "We'll die. I'll misdirect."

"Get back up! Maybe the pick up vehicle is armed! We can hide behind the trunk," he said, but Siobhan had already armed the last grenade at the base of the tree and started to run around it.

"I'll come up the other side," she said. "Get in the vehicle and move the smart rope to the other side for me."

"We could have dropped the grenade just the same," Caden said, ordering the rope to crawl to the opposite side. He heard the sounds of an aircraft approaching. He looked for it but it was not above them. Most extraction craft were very quiet; he decided this atmosphere must be carrying the sound better than he was used to.

High gravity, denser air? Or just different composition?

"This way they'll think we skirted around the tree, just like the last few times," she said. "They're tracking us."

"Tracking by what method?" he said. "If it's accurate then they know exactly what you're doing."

A VTOL braked above to come to a hover above him. Missiles launched from two pods hanging from its underside.

Fooom. Kablam!

The explosion lit up the foliage below. The crashing sound of the brittle stems echoed through the forest again as smoke rose into the sky.

That'll start some dominos falling.

Fzzzzzzt.

Caden's arm heated up from a near miss. He recoiled behind the trunk, moving away from where he guessed the fire might be coming from. His Veer suit circulated the heat from his arm, causing his whole body to warm up. Hot air escaped from his suit to be replaced with cool air from his surroundings. He started to sweat, which the suit used to dump more heat.

Caden smelled smoke. He realized the tree was on fire. *All the easier for our pickup to see us.*

"Exhale," someone transmitted. Caden exhaled.

Suddenly Caden flew upward. He grunted under the acceleration. Alien leaves and branches sliced by his face at high speed. The aircraft had launched a snatch-cable, which had hit him and pulled with little warning.

"Just you?" asked the voice.

"One more, side of the tree on a smart rope," Caden rattled off.

"I spotted her," someone said. "Bring me five meters north."

"Do we have her?" another voice asked.

"She's having trouble making it up. That branch is in the way."

"Can we clear it?"

"Negative."

"Wait?"

"No, she's down. She's down. Take us out."

Caden swore.

The simulation ended. Caden opened his eyes back in his quarters. Siobhan lay in his sleep web next to him. Caden felt a little sick.

She died to save me... like Arakaki.

His mood was shot. Siobhan opened her eyes.

"Don't do that again," Caden said. "I want to take a break."

Siobhan embraced him. She was smart enough to know what had bothered him. She did not bring out his own words against him: *It's the only thing we can do to prevent it from happening to us.*

"Later, then," she said gently. She left his quarters.

Caden decided to sleep. When he woke up, the strange mood would be gone. Siobhan was great when he needed some space. None of his other girlfriends would have done that. She was special. He did not want her to die.

19

Michael McCloskey

Chapter 3

A bright flash erupted across Jason's vision.

Kablam!

Dust and debris flew, obscuring his view of the street below. The smoke moved away in the breeze, revealing a huge smoldering hole in the street. Somewhere nearby, people were screaming.

"Yep, it's got this exit covered," Jason summarized. He fell back from the rail of the balcony and planted his back against the building.

"Okay, come back in, we'll try to get to him from in here," Imanol transmitted back.

Jason darted into the factory. He could see in his link that Imanol waited across the empty hallway. Then his tactical went out.

"Imanol?" he asked. There was no answer.

Shiny has disabled our links. And next...

One of Jason's attendants hurled into the room. Jason told his weapon to target it as he threw his head to the side. The sphere struck his shoulder.

His Veer suit absorbed most of the impact, though it hurt. The sphere rolled up his chest and found his neck. Pain arced through his body. Jason dropped and lost consciousness.

When he came to, Imanol stood above him. Jason tasted blood.

I bit my tongue again. Damn little shockers.

"Get up!" barked Imanol.

"Where is he?" Jason asked groggily. He saw some shards of metal on the floor he assumed were the remains of one or more of the attendants. He felt pins and needles across his entire body. His chest throbbed, causing Jason to imagine a damaged heart muscle.

"The floor above us, I think," Imanol said. He stared up at the ceiling. Jason assumed he was trying to line up his link view with what he could see with his eyes.

"The stairs are to the right," Jason said as he stood up. He got himself upright only to fall back against a wall.

"The right is blocked! The battle sphere blew away the entire stairwell!"

"Flank it?"

"It has no flank," Imanol said. "It's radially symmetrical, maybe even spherically symmetrical."

"Then let's get under him and attack from below."

"How? I don't see—"

"We can use a grenade to blow a hole in the floor. Hopefully right underneath him."

"You propose we attack a creature that evolved in subterranean environments and can sense us through floors by tunneling underneath it. I'm sure this'll go well," Imanol said, but he started to move.

"Well they were technically subvovokan environments," Jason said.

"Blood and souls man!"

Jason smiled through the haze of pain as they ran back through a hall and into the factory. His consciousness felt like he was floating away from his body. The pain became a distant ache.

I don't know what Momma Veer just popped into my bloodstream, but it's helping.

People cowered between storage shelves and under fabrication machines. Other forms stood still or walked calmly through it all. Those were the android bodies, waiting for their users to link back in, or walking back to the repository to await a new host. Jason glimpsed at a woman sheltering beneath a desk.

That's what you get for coming into the factory incarnate, Jason thought. *You should have just remotrolled an android from home.*

22

Jason knew what it was like: the occasional urge to actually leave the house, feel the real wind and sun on your face, or chat with friends incarnate. The chance to do something in the real world every now and then just for the hell of it. Remind yourself that there was one real world out there, at least according to the non-simulationists. Today, these people were paying for that decision.

Imanol came skidding to a halt. He pointed. "How about this?"

Jason took a look. A fabrication machine fed into an adjacent lift. The ceiling had a large trap door to allow source materials or products to be moved up to the next floor.

"Yah, good."

They ran onto the platform.

"It's not letting me—" Jason started, then the platform started to rise.

"Wow, you hacked it fast."

"Cilreth maintains a kit for us to use on low security targets," Imanol said.

She's a super valuable member of the team. I want someone to say that about me someday. Jason realized the drugs were making his attention wander. He tried to force focus. Instead he just chuckled.

"You're high as a TRB," Imanol realized aloud.

Jason laughed some more.

Tachyon receiver bases are very high, indeed.

It took six seconds to come up to the next floor, but it felt like forever. Jason felt sure Shiny would be able to detect them rising, either with his mass sense or by their footsteps. As a creature that talked with leg tapping, he might be sensitive to the vibrations in the floor.

I need to ask about that later. They watch each other talk, and use mass sense, do they also feel the hits through the ground?

23

A cover opened above to let them out on the new floor. Immediately two attendants darted in, but Jason and Imanol were ready. They did not have to aim; their weapons fired at a mere thought and handled the targeting for them.

Blam. Blam.

Hot bits of metal rained down over them.

The lift stopped. The second floor looked similar. Lines of machines sat along conveyor belts running the length of the factory. Jason heard the muttering and stifled cries of terrorized Citizens hiding from the battle sphere.

"What should we do?" whispered Jason.

Imanol made the hand signal for their 'mouse-cat-dog' tactic.

Jason pointed at Imanol, then himself.

Imanol pointed back at Jason.

I'm the mouse. Great.

It was Jason's job to lure Shiny after him, or at least distract the alien so that Imanol could get a kill shot. It did not seem as bad in his altered state of mind.

Jason peeked from cover across the second level of the factory floor. He saw nothing out of the ordinary. He cradled his weapon and moved out slowly. He did not want to get too far ahead of Imanol. He headed straight for the center of the factory floor. When he arrived in the center fabricator lane, he looked both directions. The assembly machines stood quiescent.

Think, think, think. What am I doing? Mouse.

He exhaled loudly. More of the factory lay to his right, so Jason chose that direction. He hoped Imanol had kept him in sight. From there, Jason chose a course that was a bit more exposed than he normally would have taken. As the mouse, he was supposed to be seen. The hard part was surviving being seen. The Veer suit provided some protection, but against a Vovokan it hardly seemed to matter. If the battle sphere lurked in the factory, he would just be fried again.

He scanned the machines ahead intensely. He relied upon Imanol to spot anything that might be stalking him from the rear. Jason darted ahead past another group of fabricators. He saw a large set of structures on the ceiling of the factory floor. A group of offices overlooked the floor thirty meters ahead on his right.

A robot handler's skynest.

The walls and floor of the skynest were transparent, though there were desks and platforms inside that blocked his vision of much of the interior. He paused to scan it.

Jason caught sight of a golden leg from behind a desk. He raised his laser carbine.

This thing should have enough power to penetrate the floor and that desk.

He popped a grenade off his belt and rolled it ahead. Then he started to fire into the desk.

Shiny darted out from behind the cover. Several things happened at once. Jason's grenade launched itself into the air just to be intercepted by another sphere. More spheres put themselves between Shiny and Jason. Jason heard someone yell, "Duck!"

Jason hit the deck.

KABOOM!

An explosion rocked the factory. Jason felt the heat rise painfully, then recede, though he could not breathe. His Veer suit snapped up a face mask and tried to feed him fresh air as he coughed and gagged.

"Got him," Imanol said. "Looks like you made it, though in need of hospitalization. That explosion used up your oxygen and released some toxic fumes."

"Great," Jason said, dropping from the simulation. He opened his real eyes and stretched a bit in the galley of *New Iridar*. The fogginess left his mind. Imanol was not far away, flexing his arms and legs.

"So what did we learn?" Imanol asked.

"Our coordination goes straight to conductive purple without our links."

Imanol nodded. "I agree if by conductive purple you mean straight to shit."

"Ah. Yes. That's roughly it. Sorry, core world lingo."

"We'll work on it. Anything else?"

"The real Shiny is more resourceful," Jason said.

"Sadly true. I'll make sure the TSG includes even more disruption on his part." Imanol said. He looked at the stunner on Jason's belt.

"I want you to start handling lethal weapons out of the sim," Imanol said.

"I don't feel confident about it."

"You're afraid of screwing up."

Jason shrugged. "That's just smart. You kill a friend, you can't take it back."

"We're just going to handle them and shoot them, not jump into a firefight. The fear of weapons is good, just like you said. It's like racing a motorcycle. You start out nervous, so you're careful. Then you get confident, then overconfident, and that's when you crash. I want you to lose your nerves. But don't lose the fear of handling them, that's when the accident comes."

"Okay. I agree," Jason said. "I want to learn how to fit in on the frontier."

"We're way beyond the frontier now. Besides, I can hardly teach you how to act on the frontier. You just become experienced, then you fit in."

"Then we can train. You can teach me."

Jason did not like acting like such an eager recruit in front of anyone, but he wanted to submerge his core worlder image. The only way he could do that was to learn everything as fast as possible.

"We just did," Imanol said.

"I mean, I want to know more about being out on the fringe, rather than being a core worlder."

"It's just something that comes with being someplace where everything isn't handed to you on a silver plate."

"Like what?"

"Like the recycling pipe under your fabricated habitat breaking open, and you having to crawl under there and fix it!" Imanol growled.

"What? What about the robots?"

"Maybe your *robot*, your *one and only* robot, broke that week. Or maybe your robot wasn't designed to fit between the insulative slab and the bedrock under your house. Or maybe you don't have the program handy and you have to write it yourself, and before you get it right the thing puts a couple new holes in your floor."

"On the frontier, if a robot breaks, it can't always be instantly replaced," Jason guessed.

"That's right. Often, it's the case."

"I don't know... anything about fixing things."

"No one does out of the womb. Well, not unless their parents are organized crime using neural trainers on fetuses."

"Why would you say such a thing? No one would—"

"It happens," Imanol growled. "But that's not where I was heading. I'm just saying, you just have to pick it up as it happens. Just stay calm and think it through. You'd be surprised. Doing your own plumbing on an alien world really gives you an appreciation for how long it took to perfect these mundane technologies in the first place. Core worlders don't have any respect for anything except fancy VRs and fashion, or the latest entertainer."

Imanol's diatribe had become rather harsh, so Jason decided not to say anything else.

"Your brain obviously still works," Imanol said more calmly. "You just think it through. Make some mistakes. You'll fit in just fine soon enough. Besides, like I said,

27

we're a whole new breed out here, even the frontier isn't this crazy dangerous. You'll be dead in no time anyway."

Telisa walked in.

"Hi!" Jason said.

"Training, yes? I heard crazy dangerous," she said.

"Getting ready to get someone back," Jason said.

Telisa nodded.

Did she know that already?

She sat down across from Jason and Imanol.

"There are things you weren't allowed to know as new recruits," Telisa said. "Shiny is more powerful than you may know."

They waited for her to continue.

"Shiny uses many artifacts, among them, some real Trilisk gems. The most valuable of all of them is a Trilisk AI which can interpret the wishes of sentient beings of different races and provide them. Almost magically, limited to some degree by the complexity of your understanding of what you want. We called it praying things up."

"You've used it yourself?" Imanol said.

"Yes. It's truly amazing. Shiny used it to bootstrap an industrial complex on a mineral rich asteroid. From nothing to starship construction in a few weeks. I think he brought it to Earth, though I'm not sure. I think the original Shiny has it with him at all times. He knows how to screen out the prayers of other beings. So you see, it's going to be easier to deal with him than to force him into anything. He's also used to betrayal and prepared to counter it. It's a major characteristic of his race."

"He did a number on us, for sure," Imanol said. "I understand why you didn't tell us about the other stuff. I also get now why you said we could have almost anything we wanted."

Telisa looked away. "I should have trusted you all more, and him less."

Chapter 4

Weeks later the *New Iridar* arrived at the system Shiny had ordered the PIT team to investigate. The target system had no name, but the UNSF had a set of rules for naming systems based upon their location relative to Earth. The auto-naming algorithm called it the Idrick Piper System for casual conversation, and there was a long universal identifier to go with it that no one would remember. Cilreth almost stashed the UUID away in her link cache, then decided she could just recalculate it as needed.

"Seven planetary bodies," Cilreth summarized to the team. She worked from her quarters, where she had set up a smaller version of her isolated workspace she had built on the *Clacker*. It was a sad comparison to the old one, which had made her feel like the mastermind at the center of a massive crime syndicate. Now she felt like a teenager operating out of a frontier basement.

"The target planet will be something we can visit in person," Telisa said from elsewhere on the ship. "I don't think Shiny would send us to investigate a gas giant, at least not without the means to survive there."

Cilreth eliminated most of the planets based upon their environments, leaving two candidates. She told the *New Iridar* to scan both of them. The initial summaries came through in the few minutes it took to send energy pulses out to the bodies, receive the reflections, and analyze them. Idrick Piper IV was a vast brown vat of mud. Some compounds existed there that hinted at primitive life. Idrick Piper V held vast forests and signs of a wider variety of life. Several massive constructs were spotted among the natural flora which the computer labeled as artificial.

"The fifth planet is almost certainly the spot," Telisa said. "Bring us closer."

"Scanning is a priority," Cilreth said. "Should we send down some hardware?"

"Yes. Send twenty attendants to gather details."

"So many? Aren't they a valuable resource?" Cilreth asked.

"We don't want to run out," Telisa sent Cilreth privately. "But the fewer attendants we have, the less eyes we have recording our every move. They're more than our eyes and ears; they serve as the enforcer's spies too."

Cilreth activated the attendants and sent them through the smallest lock on the Vovokan ship, which was less than a meter on a side. Telisa continued the private part of their conversation.

"I haven't really asked—"

"Yes, I'll go planetside with the team," Cilreth said. "We don't have an army anymore. And this tin can ain't the *Clacker*."

"Thanks."

"We're going to hit the jackpot and get whatever it takes to get Magnus back."

Cilreth meant it. She knew what it was like to find someone only to lose her.

The probes hurtled down toward the planet. They were too small to have their own gravity spinners, even with Vovokan technology, but since the *New Iridar* had a spinner, it did not have a high orbital speed. The attendants did not have to lose much velocity relative to the surface below, so they would be able to survive the atmospheric entry and take their places within the hour.

Cilreth kept dropping the *New Iridar*'s scans into a team feed. The PIT team would all be poring over the data. She received a request to access the data from an entity she did not recognize.

Oh. The battle sphere. Our big brother. Does it ask because it can't snoop the feed, or just to give the impression it can't snoop the feed? Or to remind me I'm at its service?

Cilreth granted the access request, then dove into it herself.

Here we go again. No doubt swarming with large predators waiting to take their turn at me. Her inner voice was sarcastic but the thought still reflected a real fear.

Cilreth saw similarities between the fifth planet's composition and that of the core planets inhabited by Terrans. Its gravity was relatively mild, and the surface was relatively warm. It had water, but only covering thirty percent of the surface. Billions of plants or plant-like creatures covered fifty percent of its surface. Huge off-white spires rose from the ground, smooth and always curved. They looked like giant ribs cutting out of the surface of the planet. These long smooth ribs held complex webs of vine-like ropes holding aloft flat organs that looked very similar to Terran plant leaves, though they were larger, about a meter in diameter.

"Vines on steroids?" Telisa summarized. "What could those pale things be? They're over 30 meters tall."

"We'll find out," Cilreth said. "Maybe those are the Celarans."

"The ribs could be a symbiotic plant that helps hold them aloft. Or even an animal," Telisa said.

Glad to see her mind is on the job. She's back into it, Cilreth thought. "The vines get big too, really big. Over a meter in diameter in some places."

"When do we go down?" asked Caden over the network.

Cilreth rolled her eyes. She wondered if the Blood Glades champ was already suiting up somewhere.

Let him get grabbed by some tentacled horror. That'll put out his fire, she thought.

"We have less hardware this time, so we're going to gather more information with the probes. Then I'll set up a

TSG that duplicates the planet's environment as closely as we can. Maybe even a few of the real critters we learn about. We can get used to what it's like down there before we ever set foot on the planet."

That's good. No need to go running around down there without some preparation. And there's no space force out to catch us this far from home. We may as well take our time.

***

A day later the PIT team had a much better picture of the planet below them. Three ruin sites had been discovered by the Vovokan scanners. Telisa opened a family of data panes in her personal view for each of the sites.

The first and smallest of the sites was dominated by a thin tower rising over 360 meters from the surface. The tower was mostly naked support skeleton except a building sat at the base and a platform rested on the top. The building's exterior shape was composed of many flat surfaces coming together at random angles. The odd construction looked familiar. Several of their Vovokan attendant spheres had converged on the site but no other buildings were visible nearby. Nothing alive or automated had been spotted entering or leaving the building.

There may be underground areas we haven't accessed yet, Telisa thought.

Telisa brought another pane in the family forward. Several native life forms had been observed moving through the forest around the tower. The pane displayed data gathered about these creatures. Telisa flipped through a series of insect analogues. The diversity of forms reminded Telisa of Terran insects. She saw all shapes and colors. Then she went through a series of rodent-sized critters. She saw a spiral-snake that could only corkscrew its way along a vine. The attendants had spotted a froglike leaf-eater whose flat, wide mouth was specialized to roll and swallow leaves larger than itself in one swallow. Telisa skipped through a few more creatures, making sure there were no signs of tech accoutrements that could indicate intelligence. She got to the largest creature.

The largest one is likely to be the most dangerous predator, isn't it? Or is that a flawed assumption? The exceptions would include very poisonous creatures, I guess. Poisons which hopefully are not effective on Terran metabolisms.

Telisa saw a meter-long thing hanging from one of the thinner vine branches. It was flat like an eel's tail or a huge leech. The vine sagged under its weight even in the light gravity. It hung from three skeletal fingers on one end. Telisa spotted three more fingers on its opposite end. She decided the top was symmetrical to the bottom, so it could probably hang from the other fingers just as easily. Its coloration was actually pretty if one ignored the shape of it. A hundred or so chevrons ran across its width on both sides of its black body. The chevrons shimmered between bright colors.

Pretty, yet creepy. Those fingers look too much like super-long Terran fingers. But it doesn't look dangerous from an objective physical analysis. Those fingers are better than huge jaws filled with sharp teeth, or an acid-belching living carpet.

Telisa's mind tried to recall what it had been like to be the flat creature on Chigran Callnir. She railed against the mismatch of memories that did not fit her current body. It was frustrating. She could remember it, yet she could not remember the *feeling* of it. Like a memory of taste as experienced by someone who had never tasted, the experiences were simply too alien.

Telisa moved on to the other pane families. The next two ruins were larger. One was a series of low buildings that had been overgrown by the native vines. The buildings were the size of Terran houses set many meters above the surface, within the vine canopy. Once again the angles were strange. She saw a lot of hexagonal components, but they seemed mashed together with little reason. Telisa realized they reminded her of the buildings in the space habitat the team had visited.

Did Shiny send us to a Blackvine colony? I got the impression these aliens had reached a higher potential than we saw from that race. Though that space habitat was nothing to sneeze at. Really surprising given the confusing clutter we found inside.

Telisa checked the output of the star to the radiation profile from the space habitat. They did not match well, but this was not expected to be their native planet, either. Maxsym had noted the light of the habitat was matched well to the Blackvines. Or had he only been talking about the windows? She decided it was too early to conclude the buildings were Blackvine. If they were, it should become apparent when they arrived.

The fauna analysis from the second site had spotted the same sorts of insect like creatures. Though she saw a new creature or two, the main thing that caught her eye was the existence of the meter long eel things with the colorful stripes. Telisa did a quick check ahead: they were at all three sites.

A dominant life form?

The last ruins site was composed of much larger buildings. Telisa's gut reaction to it was that it must have been an industrial complex. About fourteen large constructs rose to the equivalent of four or five Terran stories high. A hard pavement cover had been put over the planet's surface around the buildings. Despite some cracks it had held up pretty well. The native vines had not managed to make as much headway here as they had among the second ruin.

Telisa immediately noticed that attendants had gone missing trying to investigate these buildings.

Some kind of automated defenses, Telisa surmised. *This is the most dangerous, but perhaps the most valuable of the three sites. We'll get warmed up on the others, but this is probably the one with the greatest prizes.*

Telisa called for a face to face to discuss the data coming in. Everyone assembled quickly; the *New Iridar* was so small there was no place anyone could be that would take a long time to arrive.

"By now I'm sure you've all taken a look," Telisa opened. "We're going down at the smallest site. The tower site."

"Any ideas what the tower is for?" Siobhan asked.

"Theories only. We'll take a close look," Telisa said.

"I think it's for aerial reconnaissance of the planet," Cilreth said. "I think when these aliens came here, they set up this tower to launch and maintain their robots to fly over the planet and map part of it out in detail."

"Easily done from orbit, just as we've done," said Imanol. "Why the up close?"

Cilreth shook her head. "I don't know. The same reason we sent down the probes I guess. The vine canopy hides a lot. Maybe they needed the details. I would, if I were setting up a colony."

"They needed to collect something from the surface," Caden guessed. "It's for finding something, or harvesting things."

"They could have needed to see something coming. Something dangerous," Siobhan said. Everyone chewed on that for a moment.

"The smaller house-type buildings remind me of the space habitat," Caden said. "The shapes are crazy."

"Yes, all those weird angles," Siobhan agreed.

35

"The attendants haven't spotted any Blackvine boxes shuttling around," Cilreth said. "And I also checked for a Blackvine network. None are transmitting."

Everyone's moving rapidly ahead on their own initiative. It's a great team. If we had Magnus...

"So the similarity struck you, too?" asked Imanol.

"Yes," Cilreth admitted.

"It's not clear," Telisa said. "If there's a connection, we'll find it."

"Another interesting question is, which came first? The big buildings, the tiny houses, or the tower?" Siobhan asked.

"Don't assume they're houses," Telisa said. "Though I agree with that assessment as a first guess."

"Well, I think the big buildings show more signs of wear, so they may have been first," Cilreth said. "I don't understand why they're not all together. Three very different types of structures, isolated from each other. They're not really in three different climate zones. So why the separation?"

"What are we calling these aliens? The ones who made the ruins," asked Caden.

"Blackvines, if that's what they are," Imanol said. "Otherwise, Idricks or Pipers. Or do you prefer Idrickians?"

"Celarans," Telisa said. "The data from Shiny includes a rough line of colonized worlds cutting through this area of space. One of the systems is believed to be their origin. Celara Palnod by the Space Force naming algorithms. No Terran has ever been this far in this direction, at least, not unless the Space Force sent out scouts and never told anyone, which is vaguely possible."

"So this race is a complete blank? Shiny must have selected these systems for a reason," Jason asked.

"I think they are, or were, an advanced race. Shiny doesn't think there are any Trilisks there," Telisa said.

"He's not interested in Trilisk stuff anymore?" asked Imanol.

Telisa hesitated.

"Since it's going to be obvious soon, I'll just announce it. I'm a Trilisk clone body. Shiny sent a duplicate Telisa to lead this group. The way I see it, it just means we have a better chance to survive and succeed. The sooner you decide the same, the better."

"Knowing you're not the original gives us some trust issues," Cilreth said. Though her statement made it sound like she was questioning Telisa's position, Telisa knew it was really just to bring out the issues early to get them over with.

It will be better if we're open about this from the beginning.

Telisa nodded. "There's nothing I can say to prove anything. We live in a time when trust is impossible. We've learned about possibilities that are so amazing, yet they come with a price tag: you can no longer be sure of things you thought you were sure of before. Like who am I, really? Who can you trust, really? There's no answer I can make you accept. Whether or not you trust someone is your own decision and it's always going to come with some risk. Even if you do trust someone, how can you be sure that person next to you really is the one you decided to trust? How can you be sure they're not being manipulated?"

"It's nothing new. People have been susceptible to blackmail and other kinds of coercion for a long time," Imanol said. "Betrayal is ages old."

"But at least, in the past, they had a choice. Now we have perfect-looking duplicates, mind control, and who knows what else," Cilreth said.

No one said anything more. Imanol held a deeper frown than usual.

Is he wondering why he wasn't told before he agreed to be part of the new expedition?

"Now, I've set up some nightmare scenarios based upon the data we have coming in from the probes below. By the time you go through these, the reality is going to be a piece of cake."

Telisa led her team into training on the simulated planet. When they died, they tried it again. And again.

Chapter 5

The *New Iridar* floated down into the atmosphere of Idrick Piper V, protected from the planet's pull by its gravity spinner. As the spinner spooled down, Telisa worked with Cilreth to select a landing spot. They stood near Cilreth's quarters within earshot of each other. The others were in their own quarters or the mess, though linked into a common channel.

"There's no place to land. Should we make a spot?" Cilreth asked.

"Can't we find a clear area? Rocky plateau or anything like that?"

"Around here, no. Near the ice caps, maybe. These vine-ribs are growing everywhere and of course you saw all the huge vines. There's no clearing to land near the tower."

Telisa missed the amazing detachable feet of the *Clacker*. But she told herself she now had a light, maneuverable scout ship that would attract much less notice.

"We could try one of the other spots," Siobhan said. "They have some landing spaces cleared by the other two sites."

Telisa shook her head though no one could see her. "We can send some of our attendants to go and scout under the vegetation at some specific spots. They may be able to find a stable area, then we can settle among vines to create a clearing if we have to. The gravity spinner might tear the area up, but what other choice do we have?"

"Maybe one..." Cilreth said.

"Yes?"

"It's kind of crazy, but I found a formation that could support our weight."

Cilreth sent the team a pointer to a spot on the surface. The group took a look in their PVs.

On the surface of Idrick Piper V, not far from the tower, a pattern stood out from the random arrangement of pale spikes. Seven of the giant bone-colored structures had grown upward, then curved in toward each other in an almost symmetrical arrangement. Their ends came together at a distance less than the diameter of the *New Iridar*.

"Wow," Telisa said. "Coincidence?"

"I think so," Cilreth said. "I found a few similar arrangements with four and five spires. Their patterns are pretty random. This is just a lucky configuration, I believe."

"What if those things are hollow?" asked Caden.

"They *are* hollow," said Cilreth. "But the *New Iridar* has calculated their strength. These seven spikes can hold us. They can weather the gravity spinner, too, as long as we have it ramped down as we would on any normal landing."

"Seems dangerous," Imanol said.

"But less destructive, really, than burning or dispersing a larger area of the jungle," Telisa said.

"We could be doing something sacrilegious to the natives, if there are any," Siobhan said.

"We would be out in the open, instead of hidden in the forest," Caden warned.

Telisa waved them away. "Infinite possibilities like that," Telisa said. "No way to know which ones are meaningful. Damaging the vine forest could be just as offensive to anyone here as landing on a unique formation. We could be doing something insulting to natives just by walking out and breathing."

"Staying hidden is meaningful *to us*," Caden said.

Telisa nodded. "What about the tower itself? The landing pad on the top is small, yes, but is it strong enough?"

"Borderline," Cilreth said.

Telisa nodded. "I don't want to damage any artificial alien structure. These rib-spikes are natural, and there's millions of them. So let's land on this arrangement you found."

"Okay, here we go," Cilreth said. Then she smiled and transmitted a crash tube event across the team's link network.

"CTE? There are no crash tubes in this Vovokan shitpile!" Imanol growled immediately.

Telisa smiled despite herself. Though Cilreth was being playful, it was a solid warning. If anyone was not on the ball it would alert them to the landing.

"Should we strap in somewhere?" Siobhan asked.

"Just sheathe your swords and put down your forks, people, we're landing and it could be a crash if it doesn't work out," Telisa said. She hoped she was overstating the danger.

Telisa sat down into a chair that had thankfully been adapted for Terrans and waited. She watched the approach on the exterior sensors, as she assumed everyone was. The formation became visible below in a huge forest. Telisa saw the tower, only a couple of kilometers away.

They dropped closer. Telisa saw the huge leaves around the formations start to flutter as the turbulence and the spinner's gravity distortion started to disrupt them. Only another few seconds remained. Telisa took a deep breath and steeled herself.

I have to succeed here, for Magnus. For everyone.

The ship settled on the giant tusk-shaped spires without so much as a creak. Then the vines and leaves nearby settled. The *New Iridar* sat just a meter above the top of the vegetation all around it. The PIT team had a penthouse view above the alien forest.

"They're strong," Cilreth said. "Minimal deformation."

"Us or the damn trees?" Imanol said.

"You're always bent out of shape, Imanol," Siobhan said.

"Wait! I heard something!" Caden said.

"Landing gear?" Telisa asked.

"No, I have that—cargo bay doors are open!" Cilreth said.

Telisa spotted the Vovokan battle sphere on camera feeds from outside the ship.

"The battle sphere—" Caden said.

"Is outside!" Siobhan said.

"It's *shooting*!" Imanol exclaimed.

"Let's get out of here!" Caden suggested.

Telisa brought up her tactical combat pane arrangement. "No enemies on my screen," she said.

"It's burning the forest to the northwest... moving toward the west," Cilreth said with a calmer head.

The battle sphere used some powerful weapon to obliterate the vegetation in a long line. Telisa watched the swath of destruction grow. The enforcer machine had cleared a pie-shaped section of the forest out to 950 meters. Even the huge white trunks beyond the formation they landed upon were being incinerated. The line slowly swept clockwise toward the west.

"It's clearing a perimeter," Cilreth concluded.

"So much for our plans to spare the forest!" Siobhan said.

"Wow, that thing has a lot of juice to spare," Imanol said.

He's right on that count. This has to be costing a lot of energy.

"Could it become depleted? When it completes the circle, that might be a good time to..." Jason said.

"With what? Our pistols?" Imanol asked.

To attack it? Maybe the breaker claw. But Shiny knows I have it, and the breaker claw is more effective when the storage rings have more energy, not less. He

42

could have rigged it to explode with even more power than a normal superconductor rupture unless I got it in just the right place. If I get that desperate, I have to make sure the others are far, far away.

"We won't do anything yet," Telisa said.

Is it really afraid of the alien forest's secrets? Or did it do that to intimidate us?

The battle sphere stopped when one quadrant had been burned away.

"Cilreth," Telisa began.

"Way ahead of you," Cilreth said. "Calculating how much energy that took. If it's stopping to recharge now, that's a clue."

"I think it would hold at least 20% in reserve," Telisa said.

"One thing's for sure, it could vaporize the whole team in a second," Cilreth said.

Yes, it could.

***

Imanol took a deep breath. He smelled the air. He could not tell much about the planet's natural odor, since the smell of burnt foliage was overpowering. The seven curved spires that supported the ship had been left intact. Every other bit of material had been burned down to the near-level ground beneath. He could see the alien vegetation on the horizon.

"Nothing like the smell of plasma in the morning," Imanol drawled. He stepped out onto the fine ash. It covered the ground fairly deep, judging from how his boots sunk into the ground.

What kind of crazy mission are we on this time? Damn death machine breathing down our necks.

The Vovokan battle sphere moved around the ship in an arc as if on patrol. It moved in eerie silence. Somehow the spherical machine was clearly alien, but Imanol could not figure out what gave it away. The machine even looked Terran to his link, identifying itself with a serial number and a local name, "Escort 1". It offered no services, but Imanol had seen specialized corporate or military robots that did not publicize civilian services. If he had seen that on a Terran world before all this, would he have even noticed? Perhaps it was those strange green patterns that sometimes played lazily across its surface. A Terran machine would have had his link display an advertisement on its surface or camouflaged itself, depending on whether it was civilian or military.

"That thing has too much nervous energy," Siobhan said.

"What's DM-109 got to be nervous about?" Imanol asked.

"It's not a death machine," Siobhan said.

"True. This thing is probably even more powerful than 109."

"I meant death machines seek to destroy all life," Siobhan said.

Imanol knew she was right. Only a vengeful madman would deploy such a device. DM-109 had been such a machine in a series of entertainment VRs experienced by the masses. Imanol had never been in the VR himself, but he had heard of it. In the virtual world, the machine always started by destroying the very city in which it was constructed.

"It's concerned about aliens in the forest?" asked Caden.

"Maybe. Or maybe it's a display of power," Imanol said. "Our friend Shiny wants to make it impossible for us to forget we're on a short leash."

Imanol felt a vague fear in his gut looking at the machine. The sphere stopped and emitted a new low frequency noise. Imanol felt it in his feet.

"Blood and souls, what's that damn thing doing now?" asked Imanol. His fear came through as grumpiness.

"Seismic analysis of the area," Cilreth said. "Looking for tunnels."

"Wow. It's thorough," he said.

"Well, given that Vovokans are subterranean, I think it's second nature for them," Telisa pointed out. Jason twitched as if he wanted to say "subvovokan" again.

"Just like stabbing us in the back is second nature for Shiny," Imanol said.

No one answered him. The group spread out and tested the ground. Siobhan seemed bubbly; he recalled she was from a low grav space habitat. Imanol tested his vertical jump. His attendant reported the results: 76 centimeters.

Not bad for a ripe old man of 45 years. If it was in Earth gravity.

"It's pretty close. Feels like just a bit of a boost," Cilreth said. She did a test jump of her own.

Caden knocked on one of the round spires that supported the ship. He tried to climb it, but it was too wide and too smooth, even with a good jump and the inwards lean.

"What are those made of?" Telisa asked.

"Carbon, mostly. The structural pattern is amazing. I don't see how it grows, though," Cilreth said.

"They don't grow," Siobhan said. "They were manufactured at that size." Imanol looked at her. She was looking at some gadget and pointing it at the spire. Her attendant flew an orbit around the curved base of it.

"What?!" asked Telisa.

"Well, it's obvious," she said. "They're all the same size. All over the planet."

That never even occurred to me, Imanol thought. *Wow, I'm such a newb at this planetary exploration thing. She's right. I never saw any half-grown ones.*

"So how did they get here?" asked Caden.

"Nanomachines," Siobhan said. "Judging from their microscopic structure here just under the surface, they were manufactured in place." She folded up her device and put it in her pack.

"Well don't you have all the answers today!" Imanol said. "I guess I should just go back into the ship and take a vacation while you send back a full report to Shiny."

"Perhaps you forget this is related to my specialty," Siobhan said. "Adaptive industry applications for colonies. These ribs were created from the crust of the planet. I suspect they were all made at about the same time."

"For the vines," Telisa said excitedly. "They were made to support the vines. This place has been terraformed!"

"Celaraformed," corrected Jason.

"Amazing," Cilreth said. "I guess we should have realized that by looking at the tower. It has cords all over it. Like artificial vines. I assumed at first they were all support cables, but many of them don't add stability at all. So wherever the Celarans came from, they like vines. This vegetation is a different color than the Blackvines. Would they fit in here?"

"Creatures that live under the canopy may not be as green," Telisa guessed.

"Did you see the fauna catalog? The creatures here are specialized to the vines. So the Celarans must have brought a lot of other living things with them from their homeworld," said Siobhan. "That also explains the low biodiversity we noticed. They may have brought a minimal set of living things to achieve a balanced ecosystem, or at least one they could cheaply maintain."

"Or those things *are* the Celarans," Caden said. "What if they're still living here? Out in the vine forest?"

"Why would they?" asked Imanol. "These are their buildings, right? They would be living there."

"Unless something happened to make them uninhabitable," Jason said. "Or some kind of collapse of their civilization."

"They're aliens. Maybe they make buildings for other reasons, and still live in the forest," Telisa said. "Let's investigate and we'll learn what happened."

"Okay, let's head out. I want to see this tower in person," Caden said.

Imanol bit off a snarky reply. As fun as it was to poke the wunderkind, he was anxious to get started as well.

"Are we going to camp there?" Siobhan asked.

"I'd like to," Telisa said. "But I guess we need to see it first."

Imanol spotted the tower in the distance. It was thin and hard to see. He started toward it.

Soon the entire team was walking across the burned ground. Five Terran scout robots walked out ahead of them with a few attendant spheres. The spidery Terran robots struggled as their thin legs sank into the fresh ash. They scuttled along leaving deep rivulets behind.

Imanol did not see any rocks. He supposed they might be covered by the ash. He wondered if the battle sphere had detected any caves and neglected to mention them.

Everyone hefted a weapon. Imanol was surprised when he looked back and saw the battle machine had stayed put.

"DM-109 isn't coming with us," he noted aloud.

"So if we could find a ship somewhere else, we could give it the slip," Siobhan said.

Keeping it positive. Ah, the young.

The tower grew on the horizon as they approached. Soon they arrived at the edge of the untouched forest. The vines and their huge leaves beyond the perimeter were not even partially burned. Imanol was impressed. He did not see so much as a wilted leaf.

47

Precision as well as power. If I cut a hole through some trees with my laser, it would probably leave a black spot on the last leaf. This energy weapon was perfectly focused out to a range.

The forest looked almost the same as it did in the sims they had been practicing with. Heavy vines as thick as arms extended from the tall white tusk-shapes, branching chaotically in all directions. Imanol knew some of the vines grew even thicker, big enough to walk along. A few insect-sized things wandered out onto the burned ground in confusion. Imanol looked at them warily. He felt glad for his suit. It would take more than an average bug to bite through his flexible armor.

"Bugs. The universal constant," Imanol muttered in disgust.

The scout robots slipped into the dense plant cover and disappeared. Telisa traded her rifle for a machete.

"I'll blaze the trail. The rest of you, watch the video feeds. Cilreth, watch our six."

I'll watch your six, Telisa, he thought. He never expressed such thoughts out loud, despite his love of trolling the others. Telisa was stronger than he was and besides, how could he compete with Magnus, dead or alive? She was the leader, and a pretty good one. He had had a dozen inferior bosses on the frontier. Messing with her would force her to do something to put him in line. That would be unpleasant.

Telisa hacked into the forest with amazing speed. Her augmented body obviously provided tremendous strength. The PIT team entered the forest behind her. Soon Imanol was also marveling at Telisa's endurance: she kept going forward easily even though she had to hack every step of the way.

The huge leaves were about as thick as a finger. The cut edges oozed a sap just as Imanol would expect from a Terran plant. Imanol saw a few insects had already stopped to drink the fluid leaking from the cut vines. He carefully waved his hand in front of a few of the tiny creatures. They scampered for cover.

Okay then. Something eats them. So when they see movement, they run.

"Too bad our guardian didn't burn a trail for us," Caden said.

"Telisa will have us there in no time," Imanol said. They walked at a normal pace even though she had to clear the way.

Finally Telisa stopped to rest. Or so Imanol thought until he caught a glimpse of the tower through a gap in the giant leaves. Telisa stood before a smooth white wall. Though it had looked clean from their scans, he could now see it had a thin coat of dirt and a few stains. The wall itself looked intact. It rose at a slight angle rather than perpendicular to the ground.

Telisa started to clear a walkway around it. The building was large up close. Larger than the *New Iridar*. Whatever had made it obviously felt no need to make buildings in rectangular prisms. The wall they had found gave way to planes built at other angles within the next twenty meters. Hexagons were the most common shape among the mess. The shape generally rose from the ground and surrounded the base of the tower above, but otherwise it was crazily varied.

"There's no way in," Siobhan observed as they moved further around the building without finding any portals.

"Not from down here. I think there are openings above," Cilreth said.

"So how the hell did they get in and out?" Caden asked.

"Well, it might be this way to avoid letting critters from the forest in. To protect them. Maybe they only accessed this place by air. There is that platform on the top," Telisa thought out loud.

"Maybe they were big rats and they ran along the tops of the vines," Imanol said.

"Is that your professional opinion?" asked Cilreth.

Sure, I'll play along.

"Based on evidence," Imanol said defensively.

Telisa launched a smart rope up the side of the building. She put away her machete and grabbed her laser carbine in one hand. Then she launched herself up the side of the building with a pull from her free arm and a jump. Telisa hurtled halfway up the angled side of the building.

Imanol and Jason traded looks.

Superhuman.

Caden pulled himself up the rope, followed by Siobhan. Imanol shrugged, then turned and grabbed a vine.

"What're you doing? Is that safe?" Jason asked.

"Only one way to find out," Imanol said, climbing up. Caden and Siobhan had been climbing them since the very first of their simulations back on *New Iridar*. Imanol had done the same thing in a couple of the simulations. It was pretty easy to walk atop the biggest vines, but every now and then he would lose his balance and fall.

"Well, actually we have several ways to analyze those vines besides climbing on them," Cilreth said.

Imanol ignored her. He reached the nexus of the vine he climbed and another, thicker vine running almost horizontal to the ground. He stood up on the thicker vine and turned to cover the others as they climbed the building. He examined the tower above them.

"Those tower handles are farther apart than would be comfortable for us to climb," Imanol noted over the team link channel. "So the aliens must be tall."

"Or long," Siobhan said. "How long is the reach of a Blackvine?"

"Pretty long, I think," Caden said. "I mean, longer than a Terran's reach."

"Maybe they're not climbing rungs at all," Telisa said.

"What then?" Caden asked.

"They might only be anchor points for attaching things. Or we don't know yet."

"I like the tall theory because it's a low grav planet. So makes sense that things here would be taller, like Fast 'n Frightening here," said Imanol, referencing Siobhan.

"But they didn't come from here," Cilreth said.

"But they chose to stay here. So they might have come from a similar place. Also, they may well have adapted themselves to the local environment."

Like Siobhan did, he almost said. He caught himself looking at Siobhan fairly often. She was tall and beautiful. Terrans had been known to tweak a few genes here and there, to produce adapted locals.

Telisa came to the base of the tower. She completed a sweep with her own eyes, checking the top of the building. Imanol decided if something bad was going to happen up there it probably would have already gone down. He climbed off his perch and headed for the rope in last place.

Michael McCloskey

Chapter 6

Siobhan made it to one of the flatter roofs of the crazy building. Telisa stood waiting for her and Caden.

"Look familiar?" Telisa asked. Siobhan took a quick scan of the top of the building.

It's just like the floating space habitat buildings, except it has a top and a bottom, Siobhan thought.

"Yes. And these are just like Blackvine doors. Except these are hexagonal."

"The Celarans are Blackvines, then," Caden said. "This can't be coincidence?"

"I guess so," Telisa said, though she did not sound confident of the conclusion. Siobhan walked over to the nearest trap door. She tested it carefully. "Too many details the same. The shape has changed, but the construction of it, the resistance, very similar."

"Some of those eel-things could be in there," Caden warned. "Those doors open from either side with simple pressure, so wild animals could get in. Can't the doors lock? It seems like a useful function for any building made by any race."

"They don't look broken. It must be by design. Jam it open with something," Telisa ordered. "I'll do the same over there. If it looks clear, Caden and I will go in at the same time."

"We're not checking out the tower?"

Telisa glanced up. "I think we've seen enough from above. I've been waiting a long time to see what's down here."

Siobhan took out her smart rope and told it to hold open the door. The rope pressed the flaps open and then hugged each side to hold them. She sent her attendant into the building.

Siobhan's attendant fed back an image of a nearly empty room with white walls. The walls looked like they were covered in hexagonal white tile. Tiny holes dotted the black floor like a huge sponge. Along one wall she saw five complex metal devices. Another wall had rows of ropes or bungee cords running horizontally across the room with a meter of space between each row. She saw no dirt or dust.

It looked somehow wrong to Siobhan, though she could not put her finger on it until Caden commented.

"It's so different. There's no clutter," Caden said.

"Interesting. The only buildings this clear in the Blackvine habitat were the factories," Telisa said.

"So maybe they make something here," Caden said. "Makes sense. It's one big building."

Siobhan had not seen anything that made her think it was a factory. Adaptive industry was her area of expertise. She started looking for clues.

"If it's a factory, it's reasonable to assume that source materials would be coming in from the tower, or finished product would be lifted away from the tower. Yet none of these doors are of significant size," Siobhan said.

Telisa and Caden absorbed that speech.

"I agree, unless it was all moved in and out underground?" Telisa asked.

"Maybe through big pipes. The result of processing could be some kind of liquid," Caden said.

"But then why the tower?" Siobhan asked.

"Let's go in," Telisa said. She withheld further judgement. "Send the attendant farther ahead. Check the whole place for threats. Make sure there's no Blackvines here."

Caden and Telisa dropped down into opposite ends of the room through two doors. They held their weapons ready. Siobhan took another look around outside. Cilreth and Imanol had caught up to them. Jason stood by the tower.

"I'd like to climb up and see if there's anything interesting up there," Jason said.

I wonder if we should split up like that, Siobhan thought.

"I'll head up with you," Imanol said. "We'll drop quickly if anything rears its ugly head down here," he added, looking at Cilreth.

Cilreth took a long look at the tall tower. "Knock yourself out," she said. "I'm on lookout down here." She cradled a laser rifle in her arms.

Siobhan had to choose. The tower looked cool. It could be fun in low gravity. But she wanted to work with Caden. She dropped down into the room after him. He stood with a gladius in his hand. Telisa was examining machines on the wall.

"What's wrong?" Siobhan asked. Her hand found the handle of her shock baton.

"Nothing yet," Caden said. His sniper rifle was slung over his back and a pistol was at his belt.

"Why not your pistol?"

Caden shrugged. "You have one. She has one, and the claw. Diversity in armament."

"I think it just makes you feel safer," Siobhan told him over a private channel. "Blood Glades gladiator." He smiled.

"We have attendants and scouts in here with us," Telisa said absent mindedly. She was holding a few thin metal rods that were part of the machine on the wall. She moved them around. Siobhan had no idea what the thing was. It looked like a folded up bat robot.

Siobhan examined the tiles of the wall. Their separation boundaries were extremely thin. She reached out and touched one. The tile depressed slightly under her touch.

"Shit," she said. Caden instantly turned toward her. Telisa found her way over from the other side.

"What?" demanded Telisa.

"I hope I haven't actuated some device. This tile just moved so easily. Like cardboard."

Caden walked over. He touched another tile. Its surface was flimsy. It moved a bit. Then he pushed it further. It kept moving back, and back, until it fell through the other side of the wall. They heard a light impact from the room beyond. The hole showed the white sides of the other hexagonal prisms that fit together perfectly to form the wall.

"The wall is made of paper bricks? How could it be so flimsy?" he said.

Siobhan slid another prism out of the wall below the one Caden had pulled out. She saw one side had a crease. It was a lid.

"It's a container!" Siobhan said. "This isn't a wall, it's a stack of boxes!"

"Perfectly arranged," Caden noted. "They were so perfectly stacked I thought it was a wall covered in tile."

"Then how are these things not toppling it over?" asked Telisa. She pulled on one of the machines mounted in the wall. It slid forward easily. Telisa dug around in the boxes behind it.

"Ah. I see some support struts here where these are attached," she said. "But I think they pull right out of the wall."

"What is that thing?" Siobhan asked.

"A robot. The way it unfolds, I would say it's a flying robot. Well, a gliding one at least."

"Okay, so, those things fly from the tower, grab stuff, and put it in the funky hexagonal boxes," Caden said. "So what's in the boxes?"

For once Telisa did not warn against making hasty assumptions. She knew Caden was just voicing a theory out loud. Siobhan found the lip of the box. It opened much like a manual Terran box that could not take link commands.

"It's filled with smaller wrapped blocks," Siobhan said. "They're light. I'll open one."

Siobhan slipped a hexagonal slab out of the end. She tried to rip open a wrapper. Telisa offered Siobhan her tanto knife, but the material ripped easily. A sticky liquid leaked out.

"Watch it," Telisa said. Siobhan held it out. Telisa had a clear plastic vial ready to catch it. None of it touched them. Siobhan felt the thrill of danger.

This could be poisonous, explosive, infectious... anything.

Telisa took out an analyzer. "This will have to do," she said. Siobhan decided that meant she was missing real lab equipment. Telisa swabbed a sample and closed her eyes to concentrate on the interface.

"Well, there are a variety of molecules," she said. "Here's a familiar one, kojibiose."

"Koji what?"

"A disaccharide. This is a soup of energy molecules, I think. It's all about carbon making chains and rings with hydrogen and oxygen. I believe these are food packets. If I'm right, the Celarans are very similar to us, really, for aliens. They're carbon based life," Telisa said.

"If these really are food packets," Caden said.

"And the food packets are for them and not alien visitors or prisoners," Siobhan said.

"Highly likely. I suppose they could be hoarding poison. Or paint. Or whatever. I don't think it's coincidence. We might even be able to digest some of this ourselves," Telisa said. She repacked her analyzer.

"We don't need to know just yet," Siobhan said. "Let's not taste it."

"Caution? From you?" Caden sniped.

"You channeling Imanol?" she said back.

"We can take a look at the local herbivores and see if their bodies run on this kind of chemistry," Telisa said. "I'm betting they do. I want to capture some specimens and find out."

"*Clacker*'s labs would have made that easy," Cilreth said over the channel. Apparently she was listening in from the roof.

"I may have enough to get it done," Telisa said. "When those two come down from the tower, ask them to try and catch us some critters. Not insects; I'd like to test something larger. Preferably a herbivore."

"Will do."

"The food in the boxes may be processed. It may or may not be what the robots collect," Siobhan said. "Yes, maybe they collected this stuff from the forest. But it hardly seems necessary. Surely they have ways of mass producing food that are more efficient."

"Maybe. We think they brought these vines with them from their planet," Caden said. "So that rules out that they discovered some amazing alien substance they really wanted, right?"

"Ah yes. If we were right, this is a regular forest to them. Not alien. So if these packets come from stuff they collected from the forest, then this is a regular farming operation to them. Not a setup that collects samples for study," Telisa said.

"Okay, well I think we'll find a processing center in this building if the food was made here. Then we'll know," Siobhan said.

Telisa brought a bag out of her pack and put the wall machine into it. Then they went to a hexagonal door flap in the wall. The door was placed a high step above the floor. Siobhan noticed for the first time that the wall near the door did not have the hexagonal pattern on it.

"A real wall," she said.

Telisa nodded. "There's a scout in there. From what it sees, I think I found our processing center."

They followed Telisa through the interior of the building. Once again there was no clutter as they expected from the Blackvines. They walked past more fake walls made from boxes of the syrup packets. Tucked into the middle of the building was a large white machine built in a smooth O-shape. It was the size of a multi-passenger land vehicle. Its outer surface gleamed like new plastic or ceramic.

Siobhan immediately saw a large upward-facing intake.

"Okay, here's our processor," she said.

"Which direction is it flowing?" Caden asked.

"This way," Siobhan said, pointing.

"It's just a circle."

"Then it's filtered. Maybe chemically altered, maybe not. But it comes in from here and leaves from there."

"Well, that door right above the feed is where the tower is."

"Cilreth, could you check the base of the tower please?" Siobhan said. "Is there a door on the surface of the building inside the support skeleton?"

It only took a couple of seconds for Cilreth to answer.

"Ah yes, I see a very fine line across the surface here. There's a rail too. Lemme guess. Stuff is transported out that door up to the platform to be carried away? Or did I get it backwards?"

"Maybe both ways," Telisa said.

"Did the Blackvines eat this syrup?" Siobhan said. "I thought Maxsym said they had some kind of photosynthesis."

"He did say that," Telisa said. "But maybe it's a kind of luxury to be able to eat something you did not produce in your own body?"

"Or maybe they need it when they travel to dark places. Underground, underwater, or in space?" Caden asked.

Telisa did not comment further. Siobhan examined the beautiful white machine while Telisa and Caden searched every nook and cranny. They found only more boxes, more flexible ropes on the walls, and more of the machines Telisa suspected were gliding robots.

Siobhan got a scan of the inside of the machine from an attendant and started trying to make sense of it. Caden lost interest and moved on. She noted from chatter on the shared channel that Imanol and Jason had returned from their climb. Cilreth passed on the request to capture some animals, so they went into the forest. She felt a little nervous for them, but all she could do was flip through the video feeds of every attendant and scout they had deployed. She did not see any reason for alarm.

"What do you think?" Telisa asked her a few minutes later. Siobhan focused her eyes on her real sight and moved her PV aside.

"It's basically an extruder," Siobhan said. "If you're right, a food extruder. The contents are modestly heated, pressurized, pushed out, then cut into these hexagons, and wrapped."

"Makes sense," Telisa said. "Can you tell if it's still working? Or when it last worked?"

"Not until we figure out their electronics. Those are... well, alien. As alien as Shiny's machine control components are to us. I can tell you one thing, though, it's out of the materials used to make these boxes, and there's none of the food mixture left in there, either. Judging from the age of some suspected lubricants in this system, I'd say it's been down for less than a hundred years."

"Wow. A very recent alien presence here," Cilreth said from outside. "It fits though. I think the third installation has an active automated security system."

"Let's head back up," Telisa said. "We can join the others on their little hunt."

Siobhan touched the smooth surface before her. She had scans of everything, so the real deal was not very useful to her. She could easily build one herself if she needed to, but it would have to use her own electronics.

Telisa saw the move. "Is it well made?"

"Funny you should ask," Siobhan said. "I don't think it's perfect for this job."

Telisa smiled. "Then either the aliens aren't very smart, or..."

She's testing me.

"They've re-tasked it to do something it wasn't designed for."

"Or?"

What?

"I've made a bad assumption about what axes they optimized it upon," Siobhan said.

"I suspect that's exactly it," Telisa said. "But of course, there are many possibilities."

Interesting that she challenged me in my area of expertise. Yet I feel like she saw something there that I didn't.

"Let me study the design some more," Siobhan said. "I'll figure it out."

***

Jason and Imanol dropped back down onto the roof of the tower building. Cilreth greeted them back. Jason felt good. It was amazing to be on another alien planet. The sun and the wind and the view had lifted his spirits.

I could get used to this. The lower gravity is nice, too.

"Learn anything?" Cilreth asked.

"The rail goes all the way up. The top platform has a door there to let things through," Imanol said.

"The view up there is fantastic," Jason said enthusiastically.

"Twenty five says Caden and Siobhan will be jumping off the tower within the next 24 hours," Imanol said.

"ESC?" Jason asked.

Cilreth and Imanol laughed.

"What?"

"Frontier folk don't need your core world banks' rigged bucks. Peer-to-peer currency if you please," Imanol said.

"Frontier, peer to peer," rhymed Cilreth. It had the ring of a well known saying.

Jason shrugged. "Okay, sure, I have some. A little."

"Well you're going to need more, so don't take his bet," Cilreth said. "It was bad enough before, using UN banks. Now that Shiny's taken over, who knows?"

"Well, can you guys go out and capture some of the life forms we have catalogued with the attendants? Telisa wants to see what they digest. We think there's a food processor down there that makes some kind of syrup for the Celarans."

Imanol shrugged. "Sure. As long as we have eyes in there looking for big baddies."

Jason felt a mixture of excitement and dread. In the action VRs, the first guys to head out into the alien forest always died. He did not express his concern.

"How about between here and the *New Iridar*?" he asked.

"No, we should go out farther," Imanol said. "We may have scared some critters off on the way in."

Well, exactly.

Jason checked the attendants. There were three attendants out in the forest on the far side of the building. He hoped that would be enough to spot any major predators.

"Do you want to come with us?" he asked Cilreth.

"Me? No thanks. I'll stand here and cover you." She winked.

She has experience with what happens when you go exploring. You get gnawed upon by hideous alien creatures. Ah well, I wanted to be part of the PIT team. Now I am.

"C'mon, let's go," Imanol said. He pointed down an incline and took the lead. Jason followed him down. He sent his personal attendant ahead into the vine cover, but told it not to go far. They were able to slide off the building onto a big vine branch without using a smart rope. After that, they walked on the huge vine deeper into the forest.

It felt completely different to merge with the forest rather than follow the superhuman Telisa as she hacked through it. Jason immediately saw more insects than before. Their bodies glistened with reds and blues among the vines and leaves. Jason wondered why they were so easy to spot.

They must have predators. So they should be camouflaged. Or maybe most of them are, and I just can't see those... oh, or some might be concealed predators with body parts that look like bugs to draw something to it.

The thought made Jason shudder. At least he had attenuated to the heights in the simulations they ran on the ship. When he looked down, he no longer felt like dropping to hug the vine. The lower gravity also helped him to put fear of falling aside.

"Here are some critters. I don't have many containers, though," Jason said. "Why do you suppose the bugs are so brightly colored? Sparkly, almost."

"Who knows? We can use a bag or two to catch some creepy crawlies," Imanol said. "We could even leave some food or equipment here near the tower building to free up some storage containers. If we need it, we'll come back later."

"Something might—oh, nevermind. I guess nothing would eat Terran food."

"Dunno. Seems unlikely," Imanol said.

They went through their packs and gathered a few containers and bags. Jason also had one empty water bottle he decided would come in handy. They caught a few insect-like things.

"Here's one that can hide itself," Jason said. "These ten-legged ones can flatten themselves against the vine so much I can barely see them. The sparkly parts of their body fold in flush against the vine."

"Yeah, as soon as I reach for them it's like they disappear. And they're hard to dislodge when they do that," Imanol agreed. "Let's find something bigger."

Jason reviewed the creature catalog they had collected from attendant observations. Something seemed wrong compared to what he knew of biodiversity on other planets.

"You know, I'm looking at that catalog from the attendants. There's not that many different critters here. Siobhan is probably right. It really is like they just chose a few to bring with them."

"Could be. Or maybe we're missing a lot somewhere. This is only one spot."

"Well, any other forest would have hundreds or thousands of types of bugs and animals, right? We see here only like six small animals and like ten or twelve different kinds of bug-things."

"Well, maybe the life on Celara doesn't mutate much compared to Earth. Maybe there just aren't any chemical mutagens, or the creatures defend themselves against it."

"Isn't mutation a tremendous evolutionary advantage?" Jason asked.

"On Earth, yes. Here or Celara? I don't know. If Celara is more stable and homogenous than Earth, there could be fewer types of critters. Low disruption rates would reduce the need for life forms to constantly change."

"I wonder if intelligence would ever emerge in such a place," Jason said.

Imanol was on his hands and knees examining the vine up close. Jason swept his eyes around the forest. He did not want to get ambushed by a nasty creature.

"See these little indentations? They're along a twisting little trail," Imanol said.

"Looks like caterpillar footprints."

"Yes, I think something walked over the vine there with pincer feet or something."

Imanol produced some spherical objects from under the nearest leaf. They were orange with brown swirls.

"We should take these in."

"What are they?"

"I don't know. If I knew, I wouldn't say we should take them in. They could be plants, fruit, eggs, anything."

"I guess we have to," Jason said.

"What? What's wrong?"

"Well, you know, in all the VRs they always show up on a new planet, grab some funny looking rocks or something, they turn out to be eggs, which hatch on board the ship and whatever comes out eats them all one by one."

"We'll keep them contained."

"That's what they always say on the VRs, too. It never works."

"Well then we'll shoot whatever comes out."

"They say that too. Never works."

Imanol just gave Jason a warning look and put the objects into a container.

"A few years back on Indigo Station..." Imanol began.

"Uh oh, another story coming on," Jason said.

"Oh yah? Okay, *you* do the story this time," challenged Imanol.

"Me? You know this is all being recorded for the team?"

"Yeah so? We're supposed to be professional every second? We're only Terran. Not robots."

"Okay, well, I was recently at Stark's!"

"What?"

"I was in Stark's."

What's confusing about that? He just doesn't believe his ears.

"Stark's what?" Imanol persisted.

"Seriously?"

"Jason. What. Are. You. Talking about?"

"You know, Stark's, the famous flying dance club? Moves around all over Earth, major hotspot of famous and noteworthy Citizens?"

"No, I don't know anything about it," Imanol said.

Now it was Jason's turn. "Seriously?"

Imanol shrugged. "Must be an Earth thing."

"Well this place is super famous. There are always over a million vid feed viewers at even the dullest times."

"A million watchers? Of this club? Earthers are bored."

"It's huge. It's being broadcast to the Core Worlds, too."

"Wait. You mean someone is keeping a tachyon transmitter going with a feed from this place just so people can watch some celebs dance in another star system in near real time?"

"Yes. Totally. It's not a lot of energy by Earth standards."

"Those transmitters eat up huge amounts of power!"

"By frontier standards," Jason stopped to check their six. "Can I go on with my story yet?"

"Okay fine. So you were there. Like a tourist."

"Not just anyone can even walk in there, man. You have to be some kind of major mogul or UNSF biggie or a serious VR star. That kind of thing. But turns out, Core World Security escorted me through there."

"What?"

"Yes. They took me through there because they have a secret presence there."

"Are you on some weird drug?"

"No it's all true. My story. So this amazingly beautiful and elegant woman walks up to me and asks, 'Dance me up?'"

"What? She wanted you to dance?"

"Yes. A goddess. She must have thought the CWS escort were my bodyguards. So I say, 'I can't, I've got to save the Earth.'"

Imanol chuckled. "And it was the truth. Kind of."

"Well I thought it was the truth. So she says, 'You'd better!' and walks off."

"I wonder what she thought later when you showed up as a wanted traitor against humanity," Imanol said.

Sigh. Leave it to him to say that.

"I looked up her face. She's on the board of Guriti Nervous Integration."

Imanol opened his mouth, but Jason cut him off. "I know, you never heard of it. It's the main company putting links into kid's heads these days. Not just Earth, either. Did you know some of the latest links are installed right in the womb tanks? Before the kids even come out."

"All I know is, you better be ready to run from the CWS on your date with her," Imanol said. He stopped and pointed.

"Look! A cave down there."

Jason followed the pointer. Almost directly under the huge vine stem they stood on, the detritus on the forest floor gave way to reveal a rocky hole in the surface. It looked deep.

"Whoa. There are caves here? Under all this?" Jason asked.

"Apparently! Let's check this out."

"Bad idea, man," Jason said.

"Why?"

"There's always a cave, and it's always bad news."

"Man, you're just a rookie out here how the hell do you know it's bad news?"

"It's always a disaster in the action VRs, I mean."

Imanol rolled his eyes. *"Blood and souls,* man."

***

Telisa and Siobhan climbed back out of the building. The doors on the ceiling had no stairs or ladders, so they had Cilreth open the door and send a smart rope down. The difficult exit got them thinking again about how the creators had used the doors.

"I guess the Blackvines can reach up there and pull themselves out? Or maybe only robots came down here," Siobhan wondered aloud.

"Or maybe Imanol is right: they were tall," Cilreth said. Siobhan would have expected sarcasm there, but she heard none.

"Not Blackvines?"

"I'm still mulling it over," Cilreth said. "The Blackvines could have been living in someone else's space habitat. Or, they could have been their pet plants. I mean the possibilities just go on and on. The Blackvines could have been alien ambassadors that survived whatever killed off the Celarans. They could be conquerors fallen back on hard times after the war. Or artificial lifeforms created for entertainment."

Siobhan decided they did not have enough information to have the slightest idea what was going on yet. The picture she had been forming was made of flimsy assumptions and premature conclusions.

Siobhan caught herself enjoying the sunlight and the air of a real planet. Caden was above on the tower. He waved down at her and she waved back. Even though they could speak at any moment with their links, it felt happy to bridge the distance that way.

I probably feel so good because it's lighter gravity like home.

"Do you feel as good here as I do?" Siobhan said. "The weather's nice after being cooped up in that tiny ship."

"I always feel good. One of the benefits of being Trilisk Special Forces."

I guess someone finally said that in front of her.

That took some of the wind out of Siobhan's sails. "It's my mood, too," Siobhan said.

"I think about the past too much to be bright and cheery all the time," Telisa said. "I'm trying to focus on the work."

Change the subject.

"Speaking of... well, unique origins," Siobhan said. "Did you know Caden was a factie?"

"Yes, I uncovered that in his profile," Telisa said. "I had to investigate the current state of factory babies. It was rare to raise children away from home when I was around. Vovokans went the same way."

Siobhan had only found out on the voyage. Caden had been raised in a place where babies were made from their parent's gametes, then grown in tanks, birthed, and raised by special machines which mimicked loving parents. Some believed as the birth rate continued to drop, almost all Terran babies would eventually be produced by this method.

"He didn't arrive home until he was five," Siobhan said. "It feels so strange. He just said, when he was a kid, he didn't know the robots didn't really care about him, and when he grew up, they told him, so he just left it behind with all his other childhood beliefs like Cthulhu and the Flying Spaghetti Monster."

"Then how do they drop them off?" Telisa asked. "Robot stork?"

"He met his parents early on. They selected a custom set of mores to have him learn. His group of friends were from parents who had chosen for their child to learn the same mores. His parents came to visit about every month. They were already close by the time he was ready to leave."

"He's well adjusted and a hard worker," Telisa said. "No doubt the effects of the program. They probably had a few AIs behind that one."

"I'm a bad influence on him, no doubt," Siobhan said.

Telisa made no motions to go into the forest and collect critters with the others. Siobhan figured Telisa was monitoring Imanol and Jason and decided they did not need any help. She finally gave in to the urge to clamber up the tower after her boyfriend.

The view was as amazing as she had hoped. The alien jungle all around formed a surreal green and magenta canopy dotted with the tips of the white columns. She found it to be more beautiful than the VRs they had run. She spent a few minutes gazing around with Caden and forgot they were on a mission. Before long they were planning which spots they would jump from when they rigged together some gliding gear from ship's supplies.

An hour later, Imanol and Jason emerged from the thick vine cover with a few containers in tow.

"What did you guys find?" Siobhan asked through the link from her vantage point on the tower.

"A whole lot of nothing in the tower," Imanol said. "We got these specimens from the vines, and a bunch more from a big cave. A cave which we made it out of without incident," he added, glancing at Jason who looked sheepish.

"The view is great from the tower," Jason said. "We should make some gliders. It would be amazing to coast around in this light gravity."

"We're way ahead of you!" Siobhan gushed, then she felt foolish.

This is serious business, and we have to get Magnus back.

"That's a possibility," Telisa said, surprising Siobhan. "We found clues as to what the tower was for. Looks like they launched robots from it."

"For what?"

"The building has a food processor and stores food. A lot of food. So we think this is a farm. At the very least, it was probably used to ship the product out. It may have been used for the gathering of other raw materials as well."

"It's pretty remote," Imanol said, but for once he did not sound like he was disagreeing. "As I said, we caught a few creatures."

"I'll check what they have inside their... guts, I guess I'll call it. If these things have food inside, then we can see if it's remotely related to these molecules."

"I guess that makes sense. But it could be like looking inside an eel to see what people eat."

"And that could be confusing, since carnivores have to make glucose from protein sources," Cilreth said.

"I thought Maxsym was our bio guy," Imanol said.

"I don't see him here," Cilreth said.

"I mean you sound very knowledgeable about these things."

"I'm not," Cilreth said. "But we should be able to find what we need using our tools and we'll study the rest from *New Iridar*'s net cache. We might get lucky, and these things' diet might match up to what's in this building."

Jason held up a black bag. Something wriggled inside. "Well this bugger eats vine sap," said Jason. "I saw it sucking juice out of a thick vine stem."

Michael McCloskey

"That's perfect! Well done!" Telisa said. "Did you—"

"Yes, I got a sample of the sap," Imanol said.

"Both of you, then," Telisa said.

"We'd better head back. Our time is running out," Cilreth said.

"It's getting dark already?" Siobhan asked, looking at the sky. It was clear, but noticeably dimmer than she remembered.

"The days here are short," Cilreth said.

"We have time to get back, if we hurry," Imanol said.

"We stay here," Telisa said.

"Really?" Imanol asked.

"Yes. This place looks intact. I don't think wild creatures have been tearing through here. I'd like to get to know the place a little."

Siobhan did not like the idea much. She did not mind taking risks when there was fun to be had, but hiding in the alien building all night did not sound exciting. She traded looks with Caden. He just shrugged. But Cilreth voiced the doubts Siobhan felt.

"We don't know much about this place. Why risk it?"

"Small risk. We can get started earlier tomorrow morning. Then tomorrow afternoon we can make it back to the *New Iridar* and head over to the next ruins site," Telisa said. Everyone accepted Telisa's decision, but she continued. "Even on Earth, a lot happens at night," she said.

I wonder what she means by that. It sounds so ominous.

The team moved their packs from the roof down into the processing building. They settled in just below the doors Telisa and Caden had originally entered through. Everyone cooperated to move the boxes around to create a larger sleeping space. The ambient light in the building started to wane. As the light from the windows dropped, a gentle violet light started to emanate from the ceilings in the building. It was just enough for Siobhan to see by, though it altered the perceived colors of her clothes and equipment.

"We place scout machines just outside over our doors," Telisa ordered. Once the scouts were on guard and the attendants on patrol, everyone relaxed a notch.

"If I roll over in my sleep, I'll take out a whole wall," Imanol said, looking at the stacked boxes.

Siobhan settled with Caden at her side and a partially emptied pack under her head. They shared a look of satisfaction. Exploring an alien planet could be hard, but things had been easy so far. She peeked at Telisa. Their leader looked troubled.

If Magnus was here, we'd all be happy.

Everyone quieted down and sought sleep. Siobhan found her head filled with thoughts about the planet that died down slowly across the next half hour. She had just started to nod off when a long squealing howl came from outside. Then another.

"What the hell?" Siobhan whispered. Somehow the weird lighting made the sound more troubling. The shadows had become deeper in the building and she could not tell where the sound came from.

"Cover the entry points," Telisa said, though she did not have to say it. Everyone already had their weapons out and pointed toward the nearest doors and windows. The scout machines stood ready just outside.

The eerie sound came again. It multiplied into several similar long notes. Whatever made it, there were dozens of them. Or a hundred. The tiny cries overlapped and followed each other. Siobhan saw lights flickering out in the forest through the video feeds from their scouts.

"A flock of birds?" Cilreth guessed.

"Weird ass alien birds," Imanol said.

"Phosphorescent alien birds," Siobhan said. She saw new lights flicker and dart out among the vines.

"Too damn creepy," Cilreth said.

"I see them on scout three," Telisa said. "They look like lit darts. They're shooting around in the trees, and sitting on the houses around us, too."

The noises became louder.

"There are different sizes of them," Cilreth said. "I saw some more like a meter long."

Siobhan sat upright on edge. She breathed rapidly and clutched her shock baton.

Siobhan saw one of the shapes flit by an attendant stationed outside. She followed it across the attendant's three hundred and sixty degree vision. The creature disappeared in shadow. Then a series of stripes flickered, first white, then violet, then they were gone. Siobhan changed the wavelength range for her feed.

"I see three of them," Siobhan said. "Shift a little to the infrared. The big ones are the eel creatures. I see them hanging from those fingers, but they can fly!"

"Yes, they can," Caden agreed. "They're flat. Like gliding snakes."

They watched the creatures flit about. Siobhan saw that they launched themselves powerfully by flipping up from their three-fingered grip on the vines. Then they slithered through the air, using their flat body like a wavy airfoil. A shiver ran down her back. It got worse when she imagined the cause as one of the alien snake things sliding down her spine.

More of them started to congregate around the building. The noise rose to an alarming level. Dozens of them were hanging nearby, colorful chevrons lighting up on their bodies in rapid patterns. The others were flying about. Some of them scratched over the surface of the building.

"Are they coming in here?" Cilreth asked aloud. "There's so many!"

"Everyone, calm," Telisa commanded. "The noise is alarming. But these things aren't smashing into the building. They don't have any devices or technology on them as far as I can tell. Just a flock of alien things."

"We should have barricaded the doors!" Imanol hissed. "Are these just creatures? If they're intelligent..."

"What if they're here for the one I captured?" Jason said. He pointed at the bag. The creature inside tussled about as another of the high pitched howls came from outside. Then the sound came again, much louder. Siobhan realized with a shock one of the calls came from inside Jason's bag.

Hrrreeeeeeeeeehhhhreeeeee!!!!

"Frackjammers!" Siobhan yelped. It was *loud*. Her heart jump-started into high gear.

"Blood and souls!" Imanol added. Clearly he had been as startled as Siobhan.

Telisa walked over and snatched up the bag. Then she leaped over to one of the doors. She brought the bag to the portal and loosened the tie as she propped the door open. The eel-thing jumped out in a flash.

"It flew away," Telisa said over her link to avoid speaking through the eerie calls.

"Flew?" Imanol asked. "Or jumped and glided?"

"Not completely sure. Those things are flat and light. At the very least they glide well, as Siobhan mentioned," Telisa said.

"Maybe it's their tower then," Siobhan said.

"Anything's possible. If they can fly, and it's their building, why the gliding robots though?"

"Convenience? We hardly like to do our own farming anymore."

The noise outside began to abate. Siobhan still saw several creatures flying around the leaves, but she thought she saw fewer out there than before.

"Enough excitement for our first night," Telisa said. "We can try to seal these doors a bit better and go back to sleep. Though they haven't tried to come in."

"How could we sleep?" Siobhan asked.

"Yeah, I think it'll take an hour for the adrenaline to clear," said Cilreth.

"No, I mean, I want to watch them!" Siobhan said.

"You can watch for a while, sure," Telisa said. "But remember the attendants can record it all night. We'll be able to watch later."

Chapter 7

Caden focused on the black eel creature in his personal view fed straight from his sniper rifle sights. The creature hung from a vine by its three knobby fingers and flopped side to side lazily.

"That's the biggest one," Caden said. "I wonder if it's their leader?"

"Do you think they have a pecking order? They're not from Earth," Siobhan whispered.

Telisa and the others were studying the videos of the creatures that had flocked around the building at night, but Caden and Siobhan preferred to study the creatures in person. Telisa had tried to discourage them at first, but she had uncharacteristically folded when met with their tsunami of enthusiasm.

Caden shifted in the smart rope harness that secured him under the curve of one of the giant ground tusks. Siobhan steadied him from her own perch next to him 30 meters above the surface.

"I can't be sure. It seems reasonable that any place where you have competition for resources and mates, there would be a high probability of having a pecking order."

"Why don't two weaker ones gang up to kill a bigger one?"

"Maybe because then the strongest one doesn't spread his genes to the next generation? Or maybe the killing doesn't stop and ends up hurting the race more than helping."

"You're the alpha male of our group," Siobhan teased.

"See him flashing there? His stripes changed brightness."

"Her stripes," Siobhan said. "The females have to be larger to carry the young."

Caden did not respond though he knew she might be correct. He continued to observe.

"The flashes have to be communication. Do you think those things are the aliens that came here? Maybe their colony devolved and they went back to live in the vines."

"I would consider it likely except that the building is full of food. Yet they don't come to eat it. If they were the owners, they would probably let themselves in like we did and help themselves."

"Maybe they live in the forest because they enjoy it. The building is for emergencies," he said.

"Well, that would be alien all right."

Could they have some mystic fear of the place? Or do they know of some consequence we don't? Was there a plague? A war?

That guess made Caden worry. But he decided not to focus on fears from a random supposition.

"Let's report about the stripe flashes. We could get Cilreth working on a translation."

"Okay, but it's a tall order without the *Clacker*, I think," Siobhan said.

"It's just a shuttle, but it's Vovokan, so it must have more computational power than a Terran AI."

"It would need to observe more conversations and their circumstances."

Telisa's link channels were on a setting to discourage connections, so Caden asked for one to Cilreth instead. He let Siobhan in on the channel.

"Is Telisa available?" he asked.

"I don't know," Cilreth said.

"I thought you guys were studying the video. I think we've learned some about these creatures out here."

"Not me," Cilreth said. "I'm working on... keeping things under control."

"She means keeping the ship under our control instead of Shiny's," Siobhan whispered to him.

Caden nodded.

"Well Telisa's not answering, so she must be up to something. I'll try back later," he said. Cilreth's connection closed.

"Let's go for another glide from the tower," Siobhan said. Caden could not say no.

***

Jason was poking around the inside of the tower building when Imanol found him.

"What are you doing?" Imanol asked.

"I'm trying to figure out the alien physiology," Jason said.

"You got one of them lying around?" Imanol asked.

"No. But we have so many clues here. The interior of this place tells us what we need to know."

Imanol laughed. "A prodigy xeno scientist eh? Okay lay it on me."

Jason took the bait. "To summarize, we have: trap doors on the ceiling. These ropes all over the inside of the building. A big tower with a bunch of food at the base. A food maker. A few small robots lying around. A bunch of flat glider snake-things outside."

"I'm listening, Young Paichler."

"So, one item at a time," Jason said, ignoring the jibe about a famous deductive system from the dawn of AI.

"The doors on the ceiling. That means, they're tall, or they climb, or they jump, or they fly."

Imanol frowned, but then nodded.

"These artificial vines all over the inside. I know they're artificial vines, because Siobhan said they grew those big tusk things out there, so they Celaraformed the planet. These vines are from home. So they evolved among vines like these all around us, and brought them into their homes when they became sophisticated. So what kind of critters live on vines? Things like we saw out there. On Earth we see bats, sloths, monkeys, bugs, maybe some snakes and birds. Things that can stand on or hang from vines. They grab the vines, which means they have manipulators. Helpful for becoming advanced, no?"

Imanol shrugged. "Continue, my Paichler," he patronized.

"A big tower with vines all the way up," Jason said, pointing upwards even though the tower was not directly visible. "Food from the vines. Those eel things. All this comes together. It's clear to me, these aliens fly. They can fly out these doors, up to that tower and grab onto those ropes. They rest on these ropes in here. They eat that sap."

Jason finished and crossed his arms. *It's reasonable,* Jason thought.

Imanol cleared his throat and sighed.

"Maybe you're right," he said. "Or maybe, just maybe, these guys just hung on the vines all day long like big fat slugs, sucking tasty sap all day long. Maybe they don't move much at all. Later they built machines to cart them around like those robots we found in there. The machines can easily get in and out through the ceiling doors. Or maybe this place was built for robots only and the food maker produces their version of dog chow for their pets, or domestic animals they brought to feed on. The actual Celarans are six meters tall with fifty legs and have a triple proboscis apparatus to suck the internal fluids out of anything that moves."

Jason shuddered. The core worlds grew protein in vats to provide meat without the need to slaughter living animals, but Jason was familiar with the practices Imanol described. In fact many of the frontier worlds raised animals when the local environ could support them.

"Well, okay, I admit that's possible," he said. "I assumed the doors were for Celarans to move in and out themselves. They could be ceiling vents. Or just for the robots."

Imanol smiled. "They probably are doors. We just don't know. Let's just find some bodies or records or something that just tells us what they looked like."

Jason nodded.

A clacking sound came from the other room. Imanol and Jason turned to look.

"My link isn't showing anyone over there," Jason said to Imanol through a link channel.

"Weapons out," Imanol said, already holding a pistol in each hand. Jason took out a stunner.

I'd take out my rifle, but in these close confines, even that short barrel is a bit unwieldy.

The sound came from above. Jason heard it twice again. He saw a shadow moving. Something was blocking out the light from one of the ceiling doors.

Jason and Imanol advanced on the door side by side. Jason saw it.

"One of the eel things," Jason told Imanol through his link.

"Do we have another of those things captured in here somewhere?" Imanol asked.

"Not this time," Jason transmitted. "Why can't it get in? The doors have hardly no resistance to them."

"I don't know."

The creature launched itself off the door. Jason could not spot it, until he caught a glimpse of it flying away from one of the scout robots outside. "What happened there?"

Jason pulled the trapdoor open. "No resistance at all," he said. He examined the door more closely. He saw slots in the building where the door rested when closed. They matched up to retractable flaps on the door.

"The door has lock flaps, see?" Jason said. "They lock."

"We didn't lock any of them, not on purpose at least. You just opened it," Imanol noted.

"That door locked the thing out! It's keeping the critters out. Probably to protect the food?"

Imanol nodded. "This time, I think I'll agree with your guess. Maybe we can set an attendant to watch and catch this happening again."

"Those things make my skin crawl," Imanol said. "Like the damn Trilisk on Earth."

Jason had heard the story from Imanol's visit to the old Trilisk base on Earth. If there had been another Trilisk AI there, it now belonged to Shiny.

"I don't think we have much to fear from those things, just because they don't seem to be advanced. They're just wild animals. And not big enough to eat us, I think."

"You think. Maybe they're predators. Maybe they sucked the Celarans dry like a bunch of vampires and that's why there are no Celarans left here."

"They drink sap, supposedly. Did we get any footage of that? Anyway, I'm sure our physiology is incompatible."

"I'm glad you're sure," Imanol said. "Telisa said they were carbon based life."

I wonder what Telisa thinks about them.

***

Telisa was still in the cargo bay late in the local afternoon.

Having a Trilisk host body is a huge boost. We need this technology on Earth, Telisa thought. She had been up for days. Though she had to eat a lot, her brain was able to replenish its chemical supplies and solidify her memories without any sleep cycles. Between no sleep and a constant energy supply, she felt at least twice as effective as her old self. It was only when she started thinking about Magnus and the past that she lost focus and stopped making progress.

It was a lot more comfortable to work in the bay since the watchdog machine had moved outside to guard the ship. Telisa found herself thinking about that machine way too often compared to her mission of finding tech for Shiny to get Magnus back.

Telisa stared at the intricate robot on the table before her. She had scanned the entire structure into the computer and performed an analysis of every mechanical feature of the robot. The results were staggering. The machine had four times the mechanical configurations of anything she had on her ship of the same relative size.

"What have you learned?" Cilreth asked aloud. Telisa looked up and saw Cilreth walking into the bay.

"It's a Swiss army knife of robots," Telisa said. "This machine can walk, fly, roll into a ball, dig, swim, do all sorts of things. It has a reservoir to collect the sap, but it can also convert it into other substances and spray it. It can launch projectiles. I'm not sure what else it can do but it's a lot."

"Sensible, especially for a colony world," Cilreth said. "You would want versatile equipment when industrial capacity is limited."

"I followed up on a hunch. It's not just the robot. The clues have been right in front of us. They used food containers for walls. Turns out it's also a temperature regulation system. Even the doors in that place are like this."

"What?"

"Those trap doors. They do more than we ever realized. Those doors move air into and out of the building, and also around inside the building. They keep animals out. They adjust the light inside, charge dust particles and route them back outside, and even remove tiny organisms from things moving through them."

"Delousing doors? Nice," Cilreth said. "But I guess the big picture is, these aliens focused on things with multiple uses."

"Yes. And they made tough tradeoffs for it. This robot could fly a lot better if they had not designed it to do so much. The doors would be stronger doors if they did not do all those other things. This race does not believe in the elegant design of an object to perform just one function very efficiently."

"They must be lousy race car builders."

Telisa connected to Siobhan in a channel. She included Cilreth in the conversation.

"Siobhan, are you out there?"

"Yes? We're scouting around. We think the eel things communicate with light flashes. Those stripes on their body flicker in ways associated with their actions."

"That's good progress. When you head back in I want you to take another look at the scan of that machine in the building," she said. "You identified its function. I think there will be more than one function."

"Okay, I can do that in just a few minutes," Siobhan said. Telisa could hear her curiosity in her voice. She closed the connection.

Telisa looked at Cilreth. "There's more than meets the eye to this place. But I still haven't figured out the whole Blackvine angle."

"Can this be Blackvine tech?" Cilreth asked.

"Well, it might be. But it would be just one family of it. It's not the hodgepodge we found on the station."

"Maybe the Leonardo da Vinci of Blackvines came here and did all this on his own."

"We can't know from this place, I think," Telisa said.

"Then there may be answers in the other ruins. Those houses. I want to see if they're full of strange collections of junk, or more sweet stuff like this."

Telisa nodded. "I'm anxious to find out the exact same thing."

Michael McCloskey

Chapter 8

"They look empty from here," Telisa announced. She was using her new eye to scan the second ruins site from atop one of the artificial spires. Attendants broke away to fly ahead and take a closer look.

Cilreth waited amid the rest of the team below. Everyone was eager to take a look at the collection of alien structures they suspected were dwellings. They had landed far from the houses, aware that the battle sphere might burn the nearby jungle clear. No one wanted it to destroy anything, much less the very ruins they were here to investigate. As it turned out, the battle sphere did not burn the forest away again, though it did emerge from the ship to patrol the vicinity.

Everyone still had a lot of questions about the odd creatures that flitted through the vine forest. A day's study of the video of the night under the tower hinted that the things possessed a modest intelligence. Though the glider-eels did not seem to use tools, they did communicate with each other, either through calls or flashes of their striping, which had some form of bioluminescence. The things fed upon sap from the vines, apparently drawn in from a sharp proboscis at either end of their bodies, inside the "palm" of the three fingers at each end. No one had seen any of them excrete any waste, leading to theories ranging from waste emitted as gas to removal via the oils that protected their skin.

Cilreth kept a sharp eye out for trouble. The gliding creatures creeped her out severely. She often found herself shivering at the thought of one of the things landing on her and drinking her blood like sap from a neck artery, or attaching to her back like a giant leech.

Cilreth scanned the vines around them yet again.

I can't shake the memory of that awful thing trying to kill me.

It had been a narrow escape on Chigran Callnir Four. The nasty denizen there had almost succeeded in making her a snack. Even after all this time, returning to a strange planet made her jumpy.

Cilreth decided to try out her new link's capabilities. She set it up to suppress her fear on a three hour cycle. The emotion slipped away to be replaced by a calm acceptance of the danger. Cilreth found that she still wanted to remain alert, but no longer felt nervous about it.

Telisa leaped down from the height of the hollow spire, flipping twice on the way down as she snagged vines to slow her fall. She landed with superhuman grace, coiling up her body to absorb the impact. It reminded Cilreth of the advantage Telisa enjoyed. Cilreth admitted to herself she felt jealous of the amazing abilities, but she chose to focus on the positive side: she wasn't a ready-made Trilisk slave.

"Teams. I think you all know the divisions," Telisa said.

Telisa referred to the de facto teams they had been using during training. Once everyone picked up on Caden and Siobhan's obvious closeness, they let them train together. Imanol was Jason's mentor, which left Telisa and Cilreth as the last pair. Though Telisa had forced drills with larger teams and other partners, for the most part she did not fight it. It was fine with her as long as everyone kept learning and improving.

Cilreth received a module from Telisa. She opened it in her PV. The houses had been divided into three zones, one for each team. There was a small fourth zone directly ahead of them.

"We'll check out this starter zone as one big group," Telisa said. "If we don't see any immediate threats, we'll split up to hit these three zones. I've sent some attendants ahead as forward observers."

Cilreth added the scouts to her feeds. She saw deep green houses, rising above the vine forest floor on the huge tusk-shaped spires. Each one could hold one of the houses. She saw familiar trap doors and circular windows. Platforms ran around each house, with an orange rail around the edge. The houses tended to blend in with the forest except the rails made them easy to spot. The rails looked just like human balcony rails, except they lacked vertical support struts. Each rail was supported at only two spots on opposite sides of the house it surrounded. In many places the vines from the forest had grown around the house rails, twisting every which way and obscuring a lot of the platforms.

Those are not really guardrails like we would use them. Children or pets would go under the rail and step right off the edge.

Siobhan made the same observation and remarked on it through the group channel. "Whatever these things were, they evolved among the vines. They use them. These rails are not to hold things on the platforms, they're like metal vines ringing each house."

"Not so much a vine itself, I think, as a place for the vines to attach up to the houses," Imanol said. "That's how they get in and out. There's no way up from the ground."

The explorers followed Telisa through the overgrown vines toward the shared zone. Cilreth saw in the attendant vid feeds exactly what she had seen from their previous scouts and from orbit: the second ruins site was deserted. The vines had moved in and covered many of the houses.

These things flew. Or they were arboreal. Maybe like birds, maybe like snakes? Sloths? Chameleons? Monkeys?

Telisa cut a path toward the first cluster of three houses. The nearest one became visible, ten meters overhead, resting on one of the artificial trunks.

"Smart ropes?" Caden asked.

Telisa jumped straight up, caught a vine, then pulled herself up with her arms. Cilreth shook her head.

I should be used to it by now.

Telisa landed on the platform above, then attached a smart rope and sent it down. Caden commanded his rope to stiffen as he pointed the end upwards, then raised it slowly like an ever-growing bamboo stick. Once the far end reached the rail, it curved around and anchored itself.

"Feels pretty strong, Telisa said, testing the rail. She turned away and walked out of sight.

"You should be more careful, Telisa," Cilreth sent on a private channel.

"We are being careful. We sent scouts ahead."

"Yes well, consider, within the last one hundred years or so, this place was full of Celarans. Now it's not."

"Fair enough," Telisa sent back.

Caden had reached the top. He paused at the rail to wait for the others. Cilreth made her way up clumsily, even with the smart rope helping her by creating foot loops and gripping knobs. She looked down near the top and realized she felt uncomfortable even at this modest height.

Get back in the saddle, old girl. Glad I got my twitch today.

The others were already poring over the structure. Up close, the house was even more familiar to her even though she had spent most of her time on the ship instead of the Blackvine habitat. The outer surfaces had held up well. Everything looked watertight. Cilreth did a quick check with her link. According to their meteorological models, it had last rained here about nine or ten days ago.

Cilreth followed Imanol in through one of the springy trap doors. The door was a hexagon, with six flaps. The walls inside were a confused collection of odd angles. Black cords criss crossed some of the walls.

"Like the Blackvine habitat," Cilreth said.

Telisa shook her head. "These houses are different. Cleaner. You see it? These anchor points don't make any sense for Blackvines. They moved around in boxes. These houses were made for something that jumps, or flies, either naturally or with mechanical assistance. These houses are not Blackvine."

"But the habitat—" Cilreth started.

"The Blackvines lived in the habitat," Telisa said. "But it wasn't theirs. Think about the buildings in the habitat. They floated out in the air. They were inhabited by things that fly. Also, the farm we found under the tower. It would not be necessary for Blackvines."

"Maybe they killed the original owners off," Cilreth said. "Either by accident or on purpose. They could be conquerors. Maybe the Blackvines came here and got more of them."

"Maybe," Telisa said. "Maxsym said the windows were matched to the wavelengths they wanted. These windows are different."

Cilreth looked at the nearest window. She tapped it experimentally.

"Well, the star here is different," she said. "And they may have had different materials to use here planetside than they had when making the space habitat."

Telisa did not look annoyed. She walked over.

"I don't think the Blackvines have the social coordination to conquer anyone. We need to find more clues about what the Celarans looked like. Like maybe some bodily remains. Did they die in these houses? Did they evacuate? I'm still mulling over the possibility those creatures that flocked around us in the night are Celarans."

"Over here," Siobhan called. Everyone converged on her causing a small traffic jam.

"What?" Imanol asked for everyone.

"Behind this wall panel—a complex device. Most likely it controls the house," Siobhan said.

"Centralized control instead of distributed devices everywhere like a Terran home?" asked Cilreth. "That's interesting."

"I found at least three more mechanical items inside this wall," Jason said. "Two look like dispensers of some kind. Another might be a robot like the one we found at the farm tower."

"Wait. Siobhan, why do you think that controls the house?" Telisa asked.

"A web of tiny conductors goes from here to every square meter of the structure."

"True enough," Telisa said, sharing Siobhan's scan of the wall. "But guess what? The house is made of mutable blocks each a little bigger than our hands. Each block is not only a structural component, it's also insulation, a bidirectional heat pump, a solar cell, a computer processing component, and a sensor array. These conductors come here because that's a big battery in the wall. It's probably a centralized storage ring, harder to make that distributed like the rest of it."

Siobhan stared at the scan. "No way you can tell all that from this scan. You're cheating."

"If by cheating you mean guessing based on a few observations and what I've learned of the Celarans so far, you're right. From orbit I could see these houses absorb light differently in the morning than later in the day. Presumably without inhabitants, it doesn't take long to bring this battery up to full. I also noted before we landed that these houses keep a constant temperature. I know the doors open for us but not for those eel things. I'm guessing about the processing component part. See if I'm right."

Siobhan nodded.

"Let's go ahead and move toward our zone," Telisa said to Cilreth on a private channel. "I want to make a sweep and see if we can find something that advances our state of knowledge about the Celarans."

Cilreth sent a nonverbal agreement over the channel. The two walked out of the building onto the outside platform in the chosen direction. They stood side by side, staring at the collection of natural and artificial vines which criss crossed in a complex mess between them and the next house.

"I wish we could just jump across like at the habitat."

"We may as well use these artificial vines. Maybe it will be easier than climbing back down."

Telisa stared across the distance for a moment. "Okay, I have a route. Follow me," she said.

"Uhm," Cilreth started uncertainly. Telisa walked straight out on an artificial vine to a nearby spire, trailing a smart rope. She connected it at the destination a meter above where the vine came to wrap the trunk of the spire. Now Cilreth had one line to walk on and one line to hold on to with her hands.

"As you get to each point, tell the rope to let go and follow up behind. Toss me the ropes as they free up."

"Okay supergirl," Cilreth said, grabbing the smart rope and following Telisa.

"We're headed out into our zone," Telisa told everyone across the shared channel. Cilreth remembered to check the attendant's feed from up ahead. The Vovokan orbs revealed a collection of houses covered with overgrowth just like the one behind her. There was no sign of any living thing larger than a housecat ahead.

And that's the way we like it, old girl.

***

Telisa and Cilreth reached the last house in a rough line out to the farthest point in their zone. The house was clean and empty like the rest they had seen.

"This is the same. They all are, I think. I didn't make a list, but all this was in the other place, right? Shouldn't they vary more?"

"Depends on the norm for the Celarans, I guess," Telisa said. "Does each Celaran or Celaran living group have only the same things? Do they take pleasure in having almost identical houses?"

Telisa stood silently for a moment.

She must be checking on the others.

Cilreth checked the attendants again and spoke with the *New Iridar*. Everything seemed normal.

"I think all the houses at the second site are empty. Cleaned out," Telisa said. Cilreth could hear the disappointment in her voice.

"Wouldn't some of them leave stuff behind?"

"Terrans would. Celarans may be quite different. Besides, if each of our things had ten different functions, there would be less reason to leave anything behind. Surely each thing you had would do something you still valued it for?"

"So that tells us they had a warning. Whatever reason they left, they had time to take everything," Cilreth said.

"It's a guess," Telisa said. "Imagine a system where they had robots that notice that no one has lived somewhere for a while, so the robots come and collect the stuff. The house is certainly sophisticated enough to know if it's being used."

Cilreth shook her head.

"You always have some other theory that sounds about as reasonable," Cilreth complained. "Well how about this: what if the houses *were never* inhabited?"

"Ah, that's a good one. I don't see any wear and tear inside here. So a team of machines and specialists came ahead and set up this little town. But the rest of the Celarans never arrived," Telisa said.

"I don't know. But it seems like a good possibility. Could be anything from an accident, to a war, to a simple change of plan."

"They could still be on the way," Telisa said.

"Cthulhu sleeps. Don't even mention the possibility!"

What will they do if they come in here and find us squatting their colony?

They finished up their current house and walked out the other side. Two things happened at once. A shadow fell across them. Cilreth's emotion management suite informed her that her three hour cycle of emotion suppression had ended.

A thick roped net fell over Cilreth. Its surface felt rough on her cheek, almost spiny.

"What the—"

Cilreth crouched and looked at the edge of the net, by the rail. A long, thin leg grabbed the edge of the platform and contracted, pulling itself tight with the edge.

Some living thing is trying to catch us!

A wave of terror rose up and paralyzed Cilreth. It was as if she had never felt emotion before in her life. It smashed through her brain and destroyed all rational thought. Cilreth realized she was screaming.

Pain shot up Cilreth's left arm. She looked down and saw a thick pincer closing on her forearm. The pincer was larger than her hand. Her Veer suit was probably the only reason her hand was still attached. Cilreth's eyes resolved more parts creature amid thick net. The pinchers and the eyestalks were part of a large but incredibly thin creature. Then she understood more.

That spiny net... is its body!

"I'm not a bird you stupid thing!" Telisa said nearby. Cilreth felt Telisa struggling through the net. When Telisa moved Cilreth could feel the tension in the net altering. Cilreth thrashed, but she did not have the strength to force her way out. The pincer could not really hurt her through her armored suit, still, raw terror directed her actions.

"Cilreth! Your machete!" Telisa urged through their channel.

"What's wrong?" Caden's voice came. Cilreth realized she had screamed across all her open channels. Some part of her brain had decided she wanted *everyone* to hear and come help her.

She felt a series of sharp impacts across her back. The net tightened from above. Cilreth still saw a way out: A hole where the edge of the net rose over the rail. A buglike leg still scratched around on the platform trying to close it up. Cilreth scrambled forward, desperate to flee before the escape route disappeared.

"Stay calm. Can you get your machete?" Telisa said.

Siobhan heard the words but she did not listen. Instead she dove through the hole and right off the platform, flying head-first for the ground.

A vine hit her legs, flipped her over, then another vine flipped her again. She lost track of up and down. Light... dark... light, then impact. She landed on her stomach amid a pile of dead vines and the stubby little purple plants that grew over them on the vine forest floor.

"Hang on! We're en route!" Caden yelled on the common channel.

She heard the sounds of struggle above. Cilreth staggered to her feet. She started to run as the fear thrilled through her unabated. She ran around one spire trunk and leaped over another mound of the thick ground plants.

"We were attacked, but I've cut my way out," Telisa said over the channel. "It's still alive. And Cilreth is gone."

Cilreth approached the next spire. She dodged vines high and low. When she reached the base, she looked back to see if the thing followed.

The ground gave way beneath her. Cilreth fell again. This time, her back scraped a stone and she landed on her back, in a partially upright position. Her suit protected her. In a flash the fear was gone.

I abandoned her, Cilreth thought. *What the hell is wrong with me?*

Cilreth's eyes had trouble adjusting to the darkness. The hole above was a beacon of light. She avoided looking back up, knowing it would keep her pupils dilated.

A rustling noise came from nearby. It sounded familiar but she could not place it.

She felt fear rise again, but this time there was nothing abnormal about it. She had control. She reached for her machete but it was not there. Instead she drew her stunner.

I can control it now. And I have a stunner.

Her weapon reported readiness to her link. It had found a target. Then Cilreth lost consciousness.

***

"Cilreth! Where are you?" Siobhan asked for the tenth time. Finally an answer came.

"I'm... I fell."

Caden leaped to the next platform from his spot on a thick vine. Given the slightly lower gravity, he was able to clear the rail and land at the next house. An attendant raced beside him, ready to give him a nudge this way or that if needed.

"I have your position, just hang on," Telisa said over the channel. Even though it was not her real voice, but her thoughts sent over the link, he could tell she was busy from the choppiness of her words. "The creature is retreating now. I'm unharmed."

"Net creature? Yeech," Siobhan said to Caden on their private channel.

It wasn't a match for Telisa. I wonder if she would have made it if she was her normal old self? I doubt it.

Everyone checked their map and saw Cilreth. She was less than 100 meters away through the vines.

"There's something else," Cilreth said. Her voice sounded tired. Caden thought she sounded hurt.

"Go," Telisa said.

"Well, it's a Blackvine. It's giving me... air. Maybe. I don't know. It's saving me or killing me."

We need to get there now!

Caden made another long jump. His attendant gave him a push at the midpoint of his trajectory so he could land atop the curve of one of the trunks.

"Must be saving me," Cilreth went on. "It was not giving me anything when I went unconscious. Now it is."

"I'm at the hole," Telisa said. Caden arrived at the house where they had been attacked. He checked the position. The hole was not far. Caden had outpaced Siobhan on the way here. He suddenly felt shame.

I should not leave her behind. What if she got attacked now?

Siobhan appeared within ten seconds. She caught his worried look and smiled.

"I'll yell eight ways from extinction if some frackjammer rails on me," she told him on their private channel. "Just go help out."

Caden slipped down a vine and ran across the ground to the hole. The small plants and refuse covered the forest floor at least six inches deep.

There could be other holes we never saw.

"Could it be a trap?" Caden asked as he approached Telisa.

"I doubt it. Just keep your weapons out," Telisa said. She hovered over to the hole. Caden's attendant peeled out of orbit and plunged into the ground to join Telisa's inside.

"Cilreth!" Telisa exclaimed. Caden checked the feed. The attendant was looking at Cilreth. She lay propped up against a rock in the dark tunnel below. A Blackvine stood beside her. As Caden watched, it grasped the end of a smart rope from above in one of its tendrils and held it out for Cilreth.

It is *helping her. Maxsym was right when he said we could cooperate with them.*

"Can you believe that thing?" Cilreth said. She grabbed the smart rope weakly. It wrapped itself through the belt fasteners at her waist.

"It's not tool using? The net was part of it?" Siobhan asked.

"It *is* the net! That's its main body!"

"Impressive," Caden said. He looked Cilreth over. "Did it bite you? I saw pincers and maybe even a stinger."

"Then why aren't you asking if it pinched me? Or stung me?"

"Okay, I guess you're fine," Telisa said dryly.

"I'm sorry guys," Cilreth said. "I'm just a coward I guess. We need to get Magnus back so I can resume my job of babysitting the ship while you guys let the alien monsters chase after you."

"Next time flip on your emotion suppressor," Telisa suggested. "I found a survival trigger for natural emergencies. It can turn on automatically if it detects you're terrified."

"Yes, but... I already had mine on. It had just timed out when we got attacked."

Oh, wow. She really is struggling to do this. Not cut out for it, I guess, Caden thought.

"We need your real skills," Caden said. "You can leave the exploration part to us."

"She's a better explorer than us," Telisa said. She turned to Cilreth. "You found the Blackvine!"

"Are we going to... bring it out of there or what?" Caden asked.

"We'll see," Telisa said. "Where are Imanol and Jason?"

Chapter 9

"Let's go find some more," Imanol said.

Jason nodded. "The others are moving into their zones, too."

"You take the lead, Salesman," Imanol said. "I got your back."

"Thanks," Jason said sarcastically.

Imanol smiled. Jason was warming up to his new name nicely. Since Jason had previously interacted with clients wanting to take deep space trips with Parker Interstellar Travels, Imanol had settled upon calling him Salesman. Unlike the other crew members, Jason took Imanol's needles and never got mad. He just focused on learning. Imanol liked that, and recognized it was a good thing, because he finally had someone he could partner with.

Imanol rested his hand upon his laser pistol. He felt the weight of his projectile pistol on the other hip. Though he was joking around with Jason, he was ready to fight anything they found on short notice.

The first house in their zone was only about 100 meters and three spires away from where they stood on a platform at the edge of the shared zone. Like the others, Imanol could not resist the temptation to get there by vine instead of dropping back down and hacking through all the detritus on the forest floor. The largest vines here were as thick as his torso and branched to form a huge leaf about every three meters. He spotted one that was almost level and climbed out onto it.

"This is crazy, it's like being an ant," Imanol grumbled.

"It's a long way down," Jason said casually, in that way he spoke when he was worried about something but pretended not to be.

Michael McCloskey

"There are other vines below, plus all that crap at the bottom. And the gravity is a bit lighter. If you fall in your Veer suit, you'll be fine. Hell, by the end of the day Caden and Siobhan will be doing it for fun."

Jason stared down. "Yes, I guess you're right. Let's go for it."

Imanol moved farther down the vine. Jason climbed out after him. Imanol scanned the video feed from their attendants ahead. He did not see any dangers, yet he felt worried.

I just got done telling him this would be a breeze. Damn.

"So now I've convinced you it's safe, let me convince you otherwise. Sooner or later, something is going to get dangerous. I'm just saying, it's probably not the climbing. There's going to be a jaguar, or you know, whatever passes for a jaguar on this weird ass planet, and it's going to try and eat us. That's the best case scenario. Worst case, something smarter than us with advanced technology will kill us before we even know it's there. Possibly from kilometers away. Or more."

Jason sent the nonverbal link signal for acknowledgement. Jason paused. Imanol imagined he was checking the status of his weapons and scanning the scout's video feeds. They kept going.

At first Imanol felt wobbly on the vines and he had to keep crouching to grab a branch or another vine to steady himself. Then he started to get the hang of it, but he found himself paying all his attention on the branch below him and none of it on the other video feeds or his general surroundings. So he started to stop every thirty seconds and do a periphery check.

Within a few minutes they arrived at the next house. It looked to be in good shape. The exterior was a dark green like the others. Though its angles looked crazy, Imanol could tell it had been constructed from a lot of smaller components like the other houses they had seen so far.

"Anyone home?" Jason said behind him.

"I don't think so," Imanol said. One of his attendants was inside. It did not spot anything different about this dwelling.

"We need to do a walk through of every one," Jason said excitedly. "There has to be some clues around here!"

Imanol shrugged. "Yeah, probably. If they're all empty, I imagine Telisa and Cilreth will start tearing them all apart to examine the insides."

He pushed open the trap door and slipped in. Everything looked the same. He sniffed loudly. The air seemed clean.

Cleaners are still working. And so is this house, whoever it belongs to.

"Exact same temperature in here," Jason said. "Close to 22 C."

Imanol looked at the flexible bands on the wall and tested the strength of a couple. They reminded him of towel rods except they stretched like rubber bands. They looked familiar. He realized they had been present at the space habitat as well. It was just that they had been mostly obscured by junk there.

"It feels like a brand new home doesn't it? Or were they just really good at building and keeping everything looking new?" Imanol asked.

"I don't know," Jason said.

Imanol pictured the space habitat again. He did not think that had been as new, but he could not tell, because those houses had been so cluttered. After a few minutes, Imanol called it.

"Next," he said.

Jason reluctantly followed Imanol out of the empty dwelling. Imanol paused to plot a course through their search zone. It contained about thirty houses. He rejected the idea of a search spiral and chose a rough circle with zig-zagging perimeter.

Imanol sent one attendant way ahead to run the entire search path without waiting for them. The other three attendants assigned to them would deploy two to the next house and one trailing. Telisa had placed the old Terran bug scout robots along a route heading back to the *New Iridar* to secure a retreat path out of the settlement.

They set out. Imanol became competent though not brilliant at navigating his way along the vines. Sometimes they had to ascend or descend on detours to get where they wanted if they felt too lazy to deploy a smart rope. Imanol did not mind; it gave him a chance to experience the planet from the point of view of a native. The houses proved empty. Even Jason's excitement at his second major outing on an alien world deflated as it became clear the place was not only deserted, but very clean and devoid of interesting clues.

"There's no signs of an advanced transportation system," Imanol said as they headed to their twelfth house. "So they flew or they had flying cars, I think."

"Could be a subway," Jason said. "The entrances would be buried under all that wild growth near the ground."

Imanol shrugged.

"Speaking of wild growth," Jason said as he pointed out through the vine forest.

Imanol followed Jason's line of sight. At first he thought there was nothing but dense forest to see. Then he caught sight of some enormously thick vine stalks. The forest rose higher in that direction. Jason saw some kind of smooth green barrier like a natural membrane or perhaps a wall that was designed to look natural.

"Something odd there," Jason said. "Any ideas?"

"I don't know," Imanol said.

"Some really big vine cords coming out of there," Jason said. "The rest of that... looks like a huge husk or something."

"Yah, a big shell," Imanol agreed. The vines were so thick and dense around the shell he could not see anything else in there. "Siobhan said the tree trunks are artificial. Maybe all the vines started out like this. Some kind of giant vine egg. When they Celaraformed this place, they dropped a few of these around and they started the vines off."

"Wow. I guess I don't have any better theory. My attendant can't even get in there. It's just solid vine stems coming out of that area. They do seem to be older and thicker there than anywhere else. Maybe the vines are the Celarans? There could be a huge brain in there."

Imanol shrugged. "Then why the houses?"

"Maybe to house their alien friends, like Blackvines. Or they could even be for creatures that serve them like bees serve flowers."

"Sounds farfetched, but I can't say that's impossible," Imanol said. "With some other equipment we could scan that cluster and see if there's anything scary in there. I'll mark it down and we can talk about it later."

"You're not curious to look?"

"If the attendant can't get in there, what chance do we have? We can check it from orbit, too. I don't know. Let's take note of it, clear the houses, and see what the others think."

Jason accepted that. Imanol checked the video feeds again and kept on their planned course. The next house was in the same shape as the others so far, yet he saw it was different immediately.

"Something there. On the rail," Imanol said, drawing his laser.

Strips of cloth or plastic had been tied to the orange rail. Imanol saw yellow, red and blue. Something else sat on the platform, some curved metal snake-shape.

"Yes! Finally something worth finding!" Jason said excitedly. He pulled out his stunner and crouched on the vine.

"Questions first shoot later," Imanol said. "These are artifacts, and probably did not belong to my theoretical jaguar."

"Right."

Two attendants hovered in. Imanol saw the metal snake had two three-fingered graspers on each end. The shape reminded him very much of the gliding snake things they had seen in the trees, though this little item was not at all flattened to catch the air. It did not look like it could glide.

The attendants pushed through two trap doors and checked the interior. It looked empty.

"No one home," Imanol said. He scanned the surrounding vines. He did not see anything but vines, leaves, and insects.

Are we being watched?

Jason went forward and dropped onto the platform. He looked at the colorful strips and the metal snake, then pushed into the house. Imanol stopped and picked up the device. It flexed in his hands. The middle section was like a stiff smart rope. He pulled the graspers in different directions with each hand. The device lengthened easily.

This connects two things. Two vines? Two structural struts? Why does it look like the gliding snake-things? Maybe those damn things are the Celarans after all.

"I found something!" Jason called.

"Something new?" Imanol asked, but Jason was already there, holding out a black tube with a hole in the end. It looked like a drill without the bit, or perhaps a pistol with no handle.

106

"What is it?" Imanol asked.

"I have no idea, of course," Jason said.

"Where was it?"

"Hanging from one of those flexing racks. See this little spiral? It wraps around the rail if you hold it right there."

Imanol saw a thin black filament wrapped up into a spiral on the end opposite the aperture.

So you can hang it... I bet it would hang on a vine, too.

"It's a tool," Imanol said. He eyed the hole in the end. "Or a weapon. Don't point that hole at me."

"Of course not," Jason said. "Still, it's a danger until we learn about it. Could be a grenade for all we know."

"Then put it into the cargo carry of one of our old fashioned bots," Imanol suggested. "I think we have one around here."

"What about that grabber thing there?"

"I could be wrong, it just doesn't look as dangerous. Judgement call. I'll put this thing in my pack."

The old six-legged bots were crawling slowly through the forest closer to the shared zone. They were at an extreme disadvantage to the Vovokan attendants which could fly and hover wherever they wanted. Still, having a small carry compartment was an advantage this time.

Jason paused. Imanol assumed he was waiting for the arrival of a robot. He paced the outside platform, looking into the forest.

So many animals. There must be some predators... unless the Celarans just decided to leave those behind. I guess that makes sense. Terrans don't bring dangerous predators to the regions to be settled. We drop them on islands and place them into reserved areas far from the people when we decide to bring native species to alien planets.

Most of Earth's animal species had been preserved only as genetic samples. The destruction of the environment had brought so many animals to extinction, and only slowly had Terrans brought the creatures back. It was difficult and expensive to re-establish stable ecosystems which inevitably involved at least hundreds of plant and animal types.

Imanol saw a scout approaching on his link's overview map. He faced its general direction, trying to hear it approach. It did not work. Imanol saw the bug machine first, scuttling along on its thin metal legs. It left marks on the vine where its legs had been. Imanol guessed it had to squeeze hard to stabilize itself as it moved.

Jason met the robot on a thick vine and dropped his find into the robot's carrying hold. Then the machine turned and retreated back into the forest.

"Might as well tell it to head back to the *New Iridar*," Imanol said.

"Okay. I sure hope nothing happens to it. Can you imagine how pissed Telisa would be if we lost the only artifact around here so far?"

"Yes, it would suck, but we have a lot here. The pieces of the houses are sophisticated enough we could learn a lot. Just studying the main battery might be amazing. I don't know. I'm not much of a scientist."

"Me neither, but I'd like to learn."

Imanol suppressed an annoyed face.

Young people. Enough time and energy to learn everything in the whole damn world.

"I'm stoked to check the other houses out now," Jason said. "I was thinking we had found a big fat zero here."

Imanol nodded. He sent the attendants ahead and started in the direction of the next house. Jason led the way. The new recruit remained cautious despite the excitement of the find. He moved across the vines well enough, showing no more fear of the height, and stopped often to check around.

He's young, but not as young as Caden and Siobhan. I don't need to treat him like a kid. Well, not much longer anyway.

The next house looked empty. Jason shook his head. Imanol followed him in and they gave it a personal look just to be thorough. There were no extra possessions lying around. The inside was free of dust and smelled clean.

"What could have been different about that last house?"

Imanol shrugged. "Last ones out? Or maybe just the sloppiest ones. Or maybe they just forgot to activate the cleaning service."

They walked back out onto the house platform that surrounded the white spire holding up the house. As usual, several of the green vines had grown over the side of the house and some anchored themselves on the house rail. Imanol walked up to the rail to find a thick vine to exit onto.

"This vine has some silver parasite plant or worm on it," Jason said.

Imanol checked the vine between them. "I see something on this side too," Imanol said. "Be careful. It's moving! Damn creepy..."

Jason pulled on a vine and leaned over the rail to follow the path of the silvery vine below the platform. Then he bucked and released a strangled cry.

"What?!" Imanol saw silver lines on Jason's suited legs. He looked down at his own side of the vine and realized the extra silver vine on his side was gone.

Jason rolled off the platform and plunged. He struck one of the huge leaves, coming to a halt, then started to slide off.

"Man down!" Imanol transmitted across the common channel. He told his smart rope to crawl out of his pack while he scanned the area with his laser. He told his attendant and Jason's to try and break Jason's imminent fall. Imanol noticed his attendant refused to move.

"What?" he said out loud, staring at it. He looked down. The smart rope had not responded, either. He looked over the rail. Jason was still about four meters above the ground. He had slid halfway off the huge leaf but caught on the vine that supported it.

His suit will protect him from the fall. That thing, I don't know.

"I saw a silvery vine. Wrapped around regular vines. It's done something to Jason," Imanol transmitted. He pulled out his laser pistol and took one second to give it a target profile: Silvery tendrils.

Imanol vaulted over the rail. He caught hold of a vine in his other hand and swung clumsily, waiting for a target to present itself. He glimpsed a bulbous silver mass pulsing behind two huge leaves and told his weapon to fire. It did not respond. Imanol pulled the trigger manually. The laser blew through one, then two bursts. Imanol missed his first shot since he had not been ready for manual fire. His second shot hit. Smoke or steam sizzled up from the thing, then Imanol lost sight of it.

"Stay gone or I'll fry your ass again," Imanol called out. Jason hung limply nearby. Thoughts raced through Imanol's head.

Why haven't they responded to me? Nothing is hearing me. Are we being jammed?

Imanol kept looking into the foliage around them as he made a medical query to Jason's suit. He got no response. Imanol ran a diagnostic on his own link and found the problem: his connection capability was down.

Some kind of a trap. We're helpless.

Imanol climbed closer to Jason. He had to be careful, because the way Jason lay across the vine, if Imanol shook the area Jason would probably just slide and fall farther.

Imanol summoned his smart rope again. He stared up at the house platform and saw nothing.

"Blood and souls, how can I get anything done like this? Damn caveman style."

Imanol started to swing on the vine. He looked one last time for the silvery thing. When he did not spot it, he holstered the weapon and used his other hand to grab another vine. Slowly he maneuvered closer to Jason.

"Jason, can you hear me?"

I think he may be dead. Blood and souls!

Imanol wrapped a thinner vine around his leg and drew his pistol again. He surveyed his surroundings with his own eyes. He saw only static feeds from the attendants. Something had changed with them. Even though they could not hear his link, they had also stopped searching.

Imanol put his pistol away a second time. Then he rearranged himself on the vines.

I think I can just reach him...

Imanol stretched forward. His hand was almost to Jason. He told his suit to expose his hand, but it did not obey.

"Dammit!" Imanol exclaimed in frustration.

I can't even get my suit to open up so I can see if he's breathing.

Imanol thought of stories from the frontier about people who had died when their suits malfunctioned and would not regulate temperature or open for them. They had overheated and died inside their suits. He told himself his manual suit release was not damaged and would still work.

Imanol noticed his attendants had started to move again. They positioned themselves around Jason.

"Damn right you stupid things! He's in trouble."

One of the attendants slipped below the huge leaf and worked to stabilize it. Imanol figured it was less likely

Jason would slip the rest of the way down. Imanol just waited, looking all around for the silver creature.

A minute later, he finally received an update through his link. It had been relayed through his attendant. The positions of the other team members appeared in his PV map.

"I see them," Imanol said aloud. "They're coming this way. Probably wondering why the hell we aren't answering them."

Jason did not react. Imanol tried Jason's suit again. This time it responded with data: Jason's heart was beating. The tissue damage chart he saw open in his PV showed that Jason had some internal burns along a route through his body.

"It electrocuted you," Imanol said. "Hang on Jason. If you can hear me, just hang on."

Imanol told his smart rope to secure Jason and it finally responded.

"Imanol, if you can hear me, I'll be there in five," Telisa said. Imanol saw from the feed that she had moved way ahead of the others.

Of course. Her enhanced Trilisk body. I had already forgotten.

His smart rope wrapped itself around Jason's waist. It was anchored above on the house rail. Imanol gave the profile to the attendants and sent them on a patrol of the perimeter. Imanol decided to just wait below the platform until help arrived. He took his laser out and double-checked its target profile. He saw that it would not fire at another team member, but would shoot at unknown targets and it prioritized silvery tendrils. Imanol went into his Veer suit controls and queried about electrical resistance. The suit's operations manual told him that he could dump a portion of the suit's energy reserves as heat to increase electrical protection by freeing up some storage to absorb the offensive charge. He accepted some suggested settings.

Hot air started to flow over the surface of his skinsuit as it shed energy. Inside, the suit stayed comfortable. Imanol noticed from his energy report that his suit had more energy now than it had had when he left the ship.

What the hell?

Imanol heard a clang above. It was Telisa.

She probably leaped some superhumanly huge distance and landed hard on the platform.

"He's alive?" Telisa asked, though she probably already had the data.

"Yes. It was some silver colored plant-thing. Round, almost our size, with long silvery tendrils, at least four of them. My laser pistol drove it off."

"So it completed a circuit with his body. Probably fed from some internal chemical battery."

Telisa's smart rope secured Jason from above. Imanol did not care much about the details at the moment. Jason was alive, and the silver thing had retreated when hit with the laser. The rest of the team arrived by the time Telisa and Imanol had hauled Jason back up to the platform. More attendants flew in with them and started to patrol around the house in concentric orbits.

Cilreth took a larger medical scanner out of her pack. She attached it to Jason.

Imanol waited a long moment to hear the report. Cilreth shook her head.

"The diagnosis is electrocution all right," she said. "Some tissue burns inside his leg... the suit saved his life."

Jason muttered something. Then he yelled out.

"We got you. Don't move," Telisa commanded.

"We couldn't reach you guys. My link lost its ability to connect," Imanol said.

"Electrical attack and disabled links. Probably not a coincidence," Telisa said. Imanol nodded sheepishly. In the heat of the moment, he had not thought of that.

"My link went out too," Imanol said.

"And you took a charge," Telisa said.

"What?" Imanol checked his suit. "Oh, right, I just noticed my reserve had filled up." The suit had not been able to report the occurrence to him when his link went down. He checked the timestamps. They were both attacked at almost the same second.

"It didn't fry your links. It would have to be some kind of EM field disturbance," Cilreth said. "I can't explain it."

"Did the thing have any tools? Any signs of intelligence?" asked Telisa.

"Nothing I saw. My impression is of a carnivorous animal or plant."

"Other than being silver did it look like a Blackvine?"

"No. Not at all. This thing had a bloated body like a giant onion. No leaves or anything that looked like leaves."

Jason's eyes were open.

"Did it... bite me? Try to eat me?" he asked weakly.

"I don't think it got to you, really," Imanol said. He almost added something heroic sounding about jumping over the rail after Jason, but decided not to say anything.

"Imanol burned it," Telisa said. "He gave it something else to think about."

Jason nodded and propped himself up.

Imanol flicked through some attendant feeds and saw a Blackvine.

"Blackvine!" Imanol exclaimed.

"Ah yes, we found that one. Appears to be friendly," Siobhan said.

"Just now? Is that a coincidence?" he asked reflexively.

"I don't know," Telisa said.

Imanol almost demanded why they had not told him. Had he been out of contact that long? Then he remembered he had not reported what he found to them, either.

"We found some tools. Celaran, presumably. Though I guess they could be Blackvine."

"Where are they?" Telisa asked eagerly.

"I have a funny grasper tool in my pack. Or it's a grabbing rope, or something. It could even be a kid's toy. We put a more dangerous looking artifact into a scout and sent it back."

"Siobhan?" Telisa asked.

"We didn't find anything."

Imanol considered making a crack about the pair doing something other than searching, but with Jason hurt even he did not feel like causing any more trouble.

"I feel better now," Jason croaked.

"Let's get him back and see what we've learned," Telisa said. "We searched most of the houses today for just a few clues."

Jason pulled himself up on the platform, leaning on the rail. He could not stand up straight. His legs stayed slightly bent at the knees.

"The suit may have made sure you're not in pain, but that doesn't mean you're all patched up," Imanol said.

Jason faltered.

"Take it easy, Jason, let us help you," Telisa ordered. "Could there be poison?" Telisa asked Cilreth.

"No, it's from the electrocution," Cilreth said. "The scanner warned that there may be some delayed symptoms. I think he'll recover most of the way on his own. If there's remaining nerve damage we may need to get him back to the core worlds to fix him up."

"Dammit. I bet the *Clacker* would be able to fix him up," Telisa said.

Or Shiny's Trilisk AI.

"This will be rough going with injured. We've all been climbing around like monkeys," Cilreth said.

"Caden, keep watch for attackers. We know of at least two types now. Siobhan, go ahead with him and plot an easy route back. Imanol, help Jason make his way."

"And the Blackvine?" Caden asked.

"Cilreth and I will go back to the Blackvine and see if it wants to be our guest. As you noticed, I left an attendant to keep track of it."

"It's an intelligent being, so we should name it," Cilreth said.

"Okay, go ahead. Anyone but Imanol can name it," Telisa said, smiling.

Oh, I'll name it, all right. How about Leafy, Destroyer of Worlds?

Cilreth was silent for a moment. "Vine... Vincent. It's Vincent."

"Is Old Leafy really coming back with us?" Imanol asked.

"We'll see. We have to let Jason rest, and see if we can find what attacked you. There's some chance it was a Celaran."

Chapter 10

The PIT team clustered around the ship's mess. The ship was so small there was barely room for the entire group. Even the Blackvine named Vincent had come aboard, though no one could speak with it. Telisa stood in a doorway. Everyone focused on her.

"Okay, everyone. I gotta admit I'm getting impatient. What the hell does a Celaran look like? Siobhan?"

Siobhan looked surprised. "They look like bats. Think of that little robot you found as a Celaroid. When it's in flying form. Maybe their natural bodies can take different forms too, so it's all natural to them that everything should have a bunch of functions."

"Jason?"

Jason looked like a squid before the propeller. His face compressed.

"They look like those things outside," Jason said slowly. "You know, those things have those creepy fingers on each end. And I noticed today, all those racks on the walls in the houses, they were almost always in pairs, facing across from each other. About two meters apart. And we found the grasper tool. It looks just like those things, except it's round in the middle instead of flat. But the three fingered hands are just too similar."

"So you're saying... they hung there, one hand on each of those rails, slightly sagging across the middle," Telisa said.

"Yes."

"I also had the idea they look like those things out there, the eels," Caden said without waiting for Telisa to ask him. "In fact, the eels could be the Celaran children. A seed ship came here, dropped some machines to make a colony, and they hatched a bunch of those things, or birthed them, or whatever, from a big gene bank like facties, but something went wrong. The computers failed

117

to educate them or something, so now there's just a bunch of wild Celaran children out there running through the woods."

Siobhan laughed. "Crazy," she said, but she smiled.

Telisa smiled. "I'm impressed! Interesting ideas there. Imanol, your turn."

Imanol shrugged. "Well, I would say the net creatures and the electrical things ate them. But those things seem at home among these vines, meaning they come from the Celaran's home planet. The Celarans would not be surprised by them. So... it was something else. A predator, or a disease, or our buddy Old Leafy."

Telisa checked in on the Blackvine from an attendant video feed. It was carefully examining every bit of equipment in the bay. Telisa wondered what she would do if it caused a disruption by stealing something, or taking apart a critical piece of equipment.

"So where are our alien bodies?" Telisa asked.

"This is an advanced society. Either none of them died, or they had automated clean up," Imanol said.

"What did they look like?" Telisa pressed.

"Well, actually, you know what? I'm changing my mind on the fly. They brought those predators from their home planet. So that means, to them, they're not dangerous? That could be a clue. Either the Celarans are naturally one step up on the predator chain, or maybe they're like plants and those predators don't hunt them at all. That kind of points toward the Blackvines being the Celarans after all. Or maybe the silvery thing that attacked us. More like a plant to us than an animal."

"Cilreth said they left, and they had adequate warning," Telisa shared. "As for me, I say they never arrived in numbers. There were only a very few, like the ones who lived in the one house. The colored streamers could be children's play vines. I don't know what they look like, except they're about our size or smaller. They have vision, because they have windows. I'm thinking they're jumpers or gliders, because of the doors and, well, they grew up among the vines. So they have claws or grippers to manipulate things that came from hanging on the vines. They don't have jaws, because I think that food in the tower building is for them, so I think they basically suck up nutrients."

"You pressed us: what do they look like?" Imanol said.

"Vampire bats," Telisa said. "Flying, vine-hanging, and fluid drinking."

"The grasper device?"

Telisa was quiet for a moment.

"I think those glider snakes are the Celaran's dogs or cats. Domesticated creatures they lived with turned feral. The doors keep them out though, so they weren't house creatures. The doors *recognize* those things and keep them out. So they aren't Celarans or Celaran children. So they could be like creatures brought for food, or just things the Celarans liked."

"Well back home my door doesn't let strangers in," Jason said. "It only lets me in."

"Well, you and Core World Security, to be fair," Imanol said.

"That is strange, wouldn't it be more logical to let in things you recognize and want in, and keep everything else out? Why let unknown things like us in by default?" asked Siobhan.

Telisa nodded. "I don't know. Aliens. Either the doors are malfunctioning, or it made more sense to them to let anything in except known dangers?"

"Maybe Old Leafy hacked them out of their own buildings," Imanol said.

"Well don't despair, we still have the largest ruins site left to check out," Cilreth said. "And I'm not going to let the Blackvine hack this ship. Not that I believe that's what happened."

"Let's ask Vincent what the Celarans looked like," Jason said. "He might know."

"Obvious question: how?" Cilreth asked.

"Vincent can see. So let's use pictures," Siobhan said. "We can create a picture of us in one of the houses. And a picture of a Blackvine in one of the houses. We could put a picture of various local creatures in there, too. If we can somehow give him means to create a picture of his own, if he knows what they look like he might well draw them in the house."

"Primitive. But it's worth a shot," Telisa said. "Once we make progress we can rig some way to go high tech with it. We're not able to speak with it at all so far, even though Cilreth knows some of their over-the-wire protocols."

"The fact it moves when we're there means it's one of the insane ones," Imanol pointed out.

"Ah yes. It is aware of us, and not terrified by our existence. Which is crazy for a Blackvine, apparently," Siobhan said.

"Yep, he's a brave one if he moves around Fast and Frightening here," Imanol said.

Siobhan made an obscene gesture.

"You can teach Vincent that one first," Imanol suggested.

"See what you can do. I'll be looking at our new toys," Telisa said, heading for the cargo bay. As she walked out, she opened a private link to Cilreth.

"Cilreth," Telisa said. Cilreth connected. "I wanted to talk about your reaction to the attack."

"I know. I've been trying to think about how to make it up to you," Cilreth said.

"Just explain what happened."

"The emotion controller cycle ended a second before the attack. I had it on because... I've been feeling some anxiety on the ground. I kept thinking about that damn thing that almost killed me on Chigran Callnir Four."

Of course. I'm so stupid.

"When that thing attacked us, suddenly I couldn't handle the fear that came flooding in. The suppressor somehow left me vulnerable. It took half a minute for me to be able to handle strong emotion again, like whatever part of my mind that can control emotion had completely relaxed. It was bad timing. I didn't know it could happen. I won't use the controller on the ground again."

"I see. Live and learn."

"No. We could have died and not learned," Cilreth said.

"I know the lure of the suppressor. For different reasons. I won't use it either. If I can go without mine you can go without yours. Deal?"

"Yes."

"Actually, you should set it up for the panic trigger I mentioned. Then it turns on if you really start to lose it."

"Okay, I will," Cilreth said.

"I'll explain to the others what happened. That will help them to understand, so they won't doubt you."

"Thanks."

***

Jason met Telisa in the bay as she pored over the alien cylinder.

"Quite the toy you guys found out there," Telisa said. "Though I just started looking at it."

Jason's leg twitched a bit. The pain was a distant ache now.

"That's why I'm here. How do you figure it out?" Jason said.

"Well, we start with a few canned procedures, like an EM scanner, the spectrometers, and simple visual analysis. After that, it's a black art."

"But you have a lot of experience," he said. "Teach me."

"You can watch. This is better done virtually. You should catch up on some training I have later. I made a lot of virtual models I can give you for things to practice on. You'll kill yourself a few times."

"So this could definitely kill us," Jason said. "It looks like a weapon."

"It does," Telisa agreed. "Not sure yet."

"Well what isn't it?" he asked.

Telisa smiled. "It's not a bomb. To many complex parts and no real chemical payload. Well, I guess I should say it's not a chemical bomb."

Telisa turned it over on the table. "It also does not appear to have any foldaway arms or antennas or anything like that. As far as the outside structure, it's pretty much what you see is what you get. I thought at first it might be like the little robots we found: able to radically change shape."

"It takes power right?"

"Yes. There's a cell in it that resembles the same technology as the batteries in the houses."

Telisa sent Jason's link a pointer to her model of the device. He started to explore through its innards.

"The hole is an important part of it. Something comes out of the aperture. Not air or liquid, either, I think," he said. "I don't see any parts like bullets."

"Which leaves us with light, probably," Telisa said. "But we should keep in mind maybe it is supposed to *receive* something. We decided it was a weapon too quickly."

Jason nodded.

"Did you get a chance to follow up on those supervine clusters you and Imanol found?"

"Yes," Jason said. "We did some revisiting of the orbital scans, and sent some attendants. Though we see large vines sourced in the ground all around us, it seems the largest, oldest, and longest vine networks start from these huge husks. They are pretty evenly distributed across the planet. There's one about every 120 square kilometers."

"Well that just solidifies our theory that this place was Celaraformed. At this point, I'm willing to accept that as fact," Telisa said.

"It sure seems like it. Which makes me wonder: what was here before that?"

"Exactly. Did they destroy an ecosystem already present here? And did it have any surprises for the Celarans?"

***

Huornillel spotted an alien approaching at midday. It came through one of the square tunnels and came upon Huornillel in the metal room. It seemed likely the creature knew of her presence. It probably had a network of tools that let it track the others. Most likely including the mysterious sphere which had followed her since the aliens appeared.

Huornillel wondered how the creatures could swarm around each other and get anything done. Truly alien, they did not use any of the higher strategies of peer interaction: They neither displayed hostile confrontation to elimination, nor mutual avoidance, nor did they form dominance and avoidance pairs. Instead they irrationally kept functioning together, suffering from the n-fold division of resources available among them, essentially stifling all of them at once. They were large, sentient creatures that operated on mass consumption and side by side uncontrolled function, just like giant bacteria. It was hard to believe. Together, they were doomed to be so much less than any one of them could be individually given all the available resources.

How could they evolve like this? Hrm. Only if the resources where they came from were very high relative to their numbers. So they came from an unbelievably rich planet, or their numbers are very low. I could be looking at their entire race right here before me!

The alien was once again closely focused on Huornillel. This had happened from time to time since she had met them: they would stay close and look only at her with those odd paired light sensors of theirs. Lensed sensors, even, like some of the primitive crawling creatures of her own home planet. The poor things could probably only focus on light coming from one distance at a time!

The alien simultaneously sent bursts of electrostatic noise which Huornillel could sense with her toolkit at the same time it changed some colors on a flat surface. The alien began to emit patterns of basic mathematic principles.

I have to destroy this thing, Huornillel thought. *Otherwise, my resources will be leeched and I will be crippled as they are. These things will not flee or go dormant. Perhaps if I kill one, the others will become avoidant.*

The thing persisted. It tried some more sequences. At the same time, Huornillel heard the alien interact with its tools along narrow bands of electromagnetic emissions. Huornillel felt far superior to the creatures. This one thought Huornillel was just another tool to be programmed! These aliens had concluded they had merely to send the proper codes and Huornillel would perform tasks for them!

A moment of inspiration flitted across Huornillel's nervous system.

The aliens think they can use these codes to control me. They have that thought for a reason: this must work among themselves! They then assume it can work on me too.

This new insight expanded further: this was how the creatures shared resources without killing each other or running away: One of them used their interaction protocols to dominate the others in some complex manner that had been unseen by Huornillel. Evolution must have provided them a simple route to efficiently diverting resources to one individual. The control codes probably allowed for dominance with no need for physical violence. That way none of them risked being harmed.

Amazing. Elegant and efficient, in its own twisted way.

So this was a dominance and avoidance system after all! Except the avoidance part was not necessary. It turned peers into tools. One of them had control of the others. This was probably the dominant one before her, unless there was actually a complex hierarchy. The possibilities of such a massive system built upon the interaction protocols boggled the mind. Huornillel doubted she could grasp all the ramifications at once.

This had one very useful conclusion: If Huornillel knew how, she could program and command these creatures! As an alien she did not need to play by the rules placed upon them by evolution. Once she knew how they worked, she could use what she learned to her advantage. As an outsider she would come with none of the disadvantages. This was a very familiar concept: when a new species was introduced into a new ecosystem, sometimes it flourished rapidly, dominating the competition which had evolved together with the surrounding flora and fauna. Huornillel could be that invader.

She began to respond to the alien inputs with a new plan in mind: first, learn the protocols of inter-alien command; second, to use it to gain dominance among them.

***

"Hi. What have you guys found out?" Cilreth asked. She addressed both Telisa and Jason. The channel gained more people as Telisa hooked them in.

Makes sense. She doesn't want to explain this to everyone separately, Cilreth thought.

"It's basically a laser. An amazing laser, though," Telisa reported.

"Weapon?" Caden asked.

"It could be. Here's the thing, it's much more flexible than our lasers in so many ways."

"Fits with the Celaran theme so far."

Telisa added her vision to the channel feed and held the laser in front of her.

"This aperture can create a focus point only millimeters away. It could be used as a medical scalpel. But it will also adjust like so. Now you have a cutting laser. Or even a welder. The frequencies are amazingly versatile. I can use this in infrared as a campfire. Or heat a rock to warm us instead. And we can focus it to become a weapon like our own lasers."

"Okay, so these guys are more advanced than us," Imanol said. "We kind of already suspected that."

"It's a conceptual difference beyond that, I think," Cilreth said. "We might be able to make something like this. It would be larger, but we could do it. But we don't. Our tools are specialized. This is not. And it goes beyond what I've talked about so far. The energy cell for instance."

"Does the cell have burst chambers?" asked Imanol.

"What's that?" injected Jason.

"Our laser cells have a generic base, which lets the cells be used universally in a pinch," Cilreth said. "Such as for your flashlight under your laser there. But in order to make it efficient and effective for the laser, some amount of the cell is designed with burst chambers, one for each shot. Military designs can be eighty percent burst chambers or even a hundred percent."

"And this one?"

"No such design. The power cell has to be, you guessed it, completely versatile. Like you said before, the Celarans are making different trade offs. This device is great for a frontier site, it can be used for so many different things. But as a combat laser, it's not as good as we could make. Terrans would have ten different tools for this."

"So we've confirmed this about them," Jason said. "They're generalists, at least when it comes to their gadgets."

Telisa nodded. "That's exactly how it pans out. The robots at the tower were the same way. They were amazingly flexible, over five configurations at least. I think we'll find even more artifacts with the same properties."

"How did talking with the alien go?" Jason asked.

"Siobhan got a ways with sign language and simple link signals. The drawings didn't get anywhere. Total lack of engagement with drawings. Seems like the Blackvine would be able to see them but maybe its vision doesn't work that way. Anyway, it can understand things like, 'we want you to have this' or, 'follow me'. Beyond a few hand signals like that, they haven't gotten far."

Michael McCloskey

Chapter 11

Things felt quiet. Imanol checked the ship's status and confirmed what he suspected: they had landed near the third ruins site. The whole team was impatient for answers. Imanol admitted to himself he was intrigued as well. He now felt just as motivated as the others to figure out the Celarans.

Imanol had been reviewing the feeds from the site that had accumulated since they came to Idrick Piper V. He watched the few glimpses of Celaran robots their attendant spies had seen at the third ruins site.

The first machine was a flyer. Telisa had matched it to a configuration of the flying machine they had found at the tower in the first site. The feed showed the machine circling the perimeter of the flat area around the buildings. Imanol's gut feeling was that it was nothing more than a scout.

Imanol flipped to the next sighting. The next machine they had spotted was much larger, the size of a military vehicle. It usually moved around on four low profile treads, though at one point it simply flew over a fence. It used a powerful laser to cut away the encroaching vines around the compound, then scooped them up and moved them inside.

That's a lot of material. What is it being moved in there for? Food?

The last machine their spy attendants had spotted was smaller and circular, perhaps a meter in diameter. Its upper surface was slightly convex, rising to a flat turret on the top. Sensors hung from the lip of the device around the perimeter. It looked like an armored frisbee, and the footage showed it flying like one around the base. The video ended when the robot swerved to intercept the attendant that sent the feed. That attendant had been destroyed.

That's a security machine. It has to be. It's like a hover tank, except it truly flies.

Imanol weighed the gravity of the response. Did the destruction of the attendant mean the Celarans were hostile? Or just security conscious and diligent? He decided to leave the jury out on that one. Just in case, he loaded target signatures for each of the robots into his weapons and sent the team a pointer advising them to do the same.

As Imanol left his tiny room with his equipment, he arranged his PV to feature the maps of the compound they had targeted.

The entire area was kilometers on a side, the size of a small city. The buildings were more uniform than the houses, with sharper edges and more regular square shapes. Imanol presumed that was because those shapes had more volume for the surface area than a crazy hodgepodge of angles like the houses had. The entire compound sat upon a flat gray surface. It was probably something hard like concrete or a ceramic. A net fence surrounded the compound. The fence looked metal and connected 36 towers placed about every 200 meters.

The towers bore what looked like weapons. They were large dish-shaped projectors mounted so they could swivel and face any direction. So far, no serious weapon capability had been displayed. The dishes would occasionally swivel toward an airborne creature, causing it to swerve away. An attendant had tested the towers to determine the nature of the deterrent. As far as Cilreth could determine from the data, the tower somehow caused a force to act on a flyer and literally push it away. Whether that force was electromagnetic or gravitic or otherwise, she could not say.

An analysis from orbit had concluded the surfaces of the compound buildings and the gray surface surrounding them absorbed sunlight very well. The PIT team all agreed that was probably a secondary source of power. Any Terran industrial or military complex would need more power than could be captured from that cross section of sunlight, even at high efficiency.

No doubt about it. There will be tech here we can claim. But with those machines around, we may have to fight for it. And if there are any Celarans left here, it seems like they would be here.

The others assembled in the main bay around the same time as Imanol. He did not see the Vovokan battle sphere and assumed it had already moved outside.

"Is the sphere going to fry the jungle again?" Imanol asked.

"I doubt it," Telisa said. "We landed far enough from the compound, just in case."

Imanol took a look through the exterior feeds. They had landed the ship directly upon the vine forest this time. The ship had settled through many of them, finally resting near the surface.

The floor shifted slightly underfoot.

"The battle sphere is cutting things from underneath the *New Iridar*. I guess it wants us on the ground," Caden said.

"Should be relatively easy," Cilreth said. "We landed pretty far from any of those superclusters like Imanol and Jason found."

The team stood by. Once the ship had settled upon scorched ground, the Vovokan battle sphere moved out to patrol. Then they dropped the ramp and descended.

The air smelled smoky, but Imanol could see the forest around them had gone mostly unharmed. A trail of black smoke drifted away above.

"The smoke announces our presence," Imanol said.

"The Celarans or their machines are sophisticated enough to detect us at this distance anyway," Telisa said.

And what about anything less sophisticated but more hungry?

Vincent scuttled out of the bay after them. It moved upon several dark, leafy stalks that looked just like its arms to Imanol.

"It's coming with us?" Imanol asked slowly.

"Vincent's not our prisoner," Telisa said.

"Okay. Creepy."

I hope Telisa's not ready to make the same old mistakes again. Trusting aliens hasn't worked out well for us.

As if reading his mind, Telisa spoke up again.

"I know we can't trust Vincent. I also know, we stand to learn a lot from him. He's not Shiny. If we can communicate, chances are Vincent knows a thing or two about the Celarans."

"Which would be a thing or two more than we know," Siobhan said glumly.

"Oh we have some ideas," Jason said.

Imanol looked at Jason. His partner seemed to be taking the accompanying alien plant well. As for himself... Imanol had added Old Leafy to his weapon target sigs long ago.

Wait till the damn plant tries to eat him like that other thing. Then he'll get a healthy sense of paranoia and cynicism.

Jason caught his look. "I'm okay. It was some kind of wild animal that attacked us, I think. Your jaguar. Vincent here is an intelligent creature."

"Which makes him more dangerous, not less," grumbled Imanol.

He sounded like the old Telisa. Too trusting.

Jason did not reply. Imanol decided he had caused enough trouble and focused on the task at hand. He looked at his link map and oriented himself relative to the complex.

Telisa took the lead again. She walked over to the edge of the undergrowth and brought her arm back to start hacking, but Siobhan interrupted her.

"Let's just climb instead. We can get a view from above, and avoid any more holes in the ground."

"Is that what the rest of you want to do?"

"Yes," Caden said.

Well, of course.

"I'm not such a good climber, but I could use the practice I guess," Cilreth said. She sounded a lot less enthused about the idea, like Imanol himself.

"Yes, fine, we'll play up there with the young'uns," he said grumpily.

The team took to the vines like a bunch of kids. Caden and Siobhan, at least, were just kids as far as Imanol thought. They climbed up and started along a huge vine heading in roughly the right direction. He saw Jason take a smart rope out of his pack and hand it to Vincent. The Blackvine reached out and took the cluster of black rope.

"Does it know about our link interfaces?" Imanol asked.

"Vincent? He's been playing with them, but hasn't figured them out yet," Cilreth said.

"Don't give him too many permissions!" Imanol blurted.

"Of course not," Cilreth said on a private channel. "Us veterans will keep these kids in line."

Imanol nodded.

"I gave him permission for the smart rope," Jason said.

"Okay," Telisa said. "Just that for now."

Vincent's smart rope jumped and coiled at random. Telisa took her rope out and prepared to demonstrate. She paused.

"Hrm. The link protocols aren't set up to send messages in the open. Vincent sees only encrypted signals.

And I can't add him to the channel to let him see the conversation with the rope unobscured."

"It would be too dangerous to let him clone your link," Siobhan said. "Besides the commands all have a time-component to the authentication. He can't just copy your same commands a second later and get it to work."

"I'll fix it," Cilreth said.

"How?" Telisa and Siobhan asked simultaneously.

"I'll give him a link. I can set it up as a repeater. He can transmit commands to his link and it will establish his secure connections. We'll authorize him to do a few things here and there."

"You have spare links lying around?" asked Imanol. He knew it was illegal to have links other than your own unless you were an authorized entity that installed them in people. Of course, he had seen it on the frontier before—and they were now way beyond that.

"I picked up some, yes," she said. "If you recall, things were kind of busy last time we made it home. That opened some opportunities. Given we're on the outs with the... well, we were working against the previous government, and now, maybe the new one, too."

Wow. Connected.

Imanol checked Telisa's face. He gauged that she already knew about the links.

"I wish we had thought about this earlier," Caden said.

"Give me fifteen minutes," Cilreth said, running back inside.

"Bring some camping gear. We probably won't be able to just walk in and sleepover this time," Telisa said.

"What's the plan, exactly?" Imanol asked.

"We'll take a look around. Our scouts have never been bothered off the flat area that surrounds the buildings. There's a fence of sorts, beyond that, our machines have been attacked. So we'll set up a temporary camp just outside the fence. Then, Siobhan and I will go in cloaked and see what we can find out."

Imanol walked back in to fill another pack since he had to wait anyway. Knowing they would have a temporary camp opened up new possibilities. He could take some extra food, water, and equipment, knowing he would not have to carry the whole thing far.

I'll pack like Maxsym, he thought. Imanol realized he actually felt sorry for the once-PIT member. He had died on the *Clacker* when Shiny backstabbed them. Poor guy had never had a chance.

Who else has PIT lost? Quite a few. Arakaki. Magnus, sort of. And the original guys, Jack and... Thomas? There were more. Telisa doesn't talk about it much. Kinda puts a damper on recruiting I bet.

Once Imanol had his pack and returned, Cilreth was outside and working with a link. Everyone tried not to watch her, even though they were all waiting. Finally Cilreth handed the small device to Vincent. The Blackvine accepted it.

"The rope is the only service he has available to start," she said.

The rope started to move. It performed some random maneuvers, this time with clear purpose and nothing like the spastic twitching from before.

"Let's move out. Vincent can stay here and play all it wants," Imanol said.

Telisa shrugged. She leaped straight up, caught a big vine above and swung up onto it. Everyone else started to follow more slowly. No one else on the team could match her feat of strength. Once on her perch, Telisa moved slowly forward, scanning for danger while everyone else made it to the huge branch of the vine. Vincent followed along last. It had stowed the smart rope among its dark tendrils.

Nothing threatened them as they climbed away from *New Iridar* toward the third site. Telisa kept the attendant spheres from wandering onto the flat surfaces ahead so they would not get lost like the others. She picked a big vine that approached their goal and followed it up to the top of one of the huge artificial spires that rose from the ground.

Telisa stopped to take a look. Caden arrived next, then Imanol. The vine wrapped around the spire, providing a solid ledge with a great view of the compound. Imanol paused with the others to look out over the alien buildings.

Their gray surfaces looked clear. There were not many windows. To Imanol, the large buildings looked a lot like spacecraft hangars.

If we got a Celaran space ship, that would please Shiny. Maybe Telisa could get on his good side and snag Magnus back. Then we could go back out on a mission and just run like hell.

"This is our new camp," Telisa announced. "At the base of this spire."

"Should we camouflage it?" Caden asked.

"If you want to design it with that in mind, fine, but don't work too hard. At their technology level, I imagine those machines would spot us anyway, if they're searching for a threat."

"Okay," Caden said. He took out a smart rope and told it to head down. Imanol joined Caden. He was eager to get rid of the extra weight he had been carrying.

As Caden and Imanol cleared the ground around the trunk of the spire, the conversation continued up on the overlook. The two at ground level listened in on the group channel.

"So what's the plan?" Siobhan asked. "We go in first? What if they shoot?"

"We can't risk just walking in. They took steps to keep our robots out. You and I will go in stealthed."

"I'm ready." Imanol could hear the excitement in Siobhan's voice.

She's looking for another danger high and Telisa's dropping one right on her lap.

Imanol caught a worried look cross Caden's face.

So he does have enough sense to know she might not come back.

Imanol thought about Caden and Siobhan. He knew it was tragic. Siobhan would get killed sooner or later, or Caden would, then the survivor would take another big step in the transformation from young and carefree into a mature cynic like Telisa or Imanol.

It would almost be luckier if they both die together. More romantic, too, he thought.

"Talk to Fast and Frightening," Imanol found himself saying to Caden. "Tell her it's not a game. Tell her to grow up so you two can make it to thirty together." For once his voice was flat and sincere.

Caden sensed that Imanol was not giving him a hard time. He nodded.

Michael McCloskey

Chapter 12

"We'll cut through the fence here," Telisa said to Siobhan. They crouched beside the base of a large vine near the edge of the Celaran compound. Three huge leaves drooped down over them, forming a concealed niche from which they would deploy.

Telisa used their shared link map to mark a section of the fence between two Celaran towers directly before them.

"I want to move in quickly, because I think one of those big machines that clears the forest will come out to repair it. I'm guessing these machines are as multi role as the Celaran tools."

Siobhan nodded. She looked pensive. Something had changed in her attitude.

This isn't the rip-roaring to go Fast and Frightening that I know.

"What is it?" Telisa asked.

"Uhm... I want to take it more by the book this time," she said. "Minimal risk, okay?"

"Yes. That's okay. There's no book, though. This isn't the Space Force. Today, it's just, anything happens, you get the hell out of there, got it?"

"Thanks. I don't mean to let you down. It's just..."

"You have something to lose now? That's fine. I get it. We want a look today. That's it. You take a look, you get out, work done."

Siobhan sent her the nonverbal link acknowledgement.

"Me first," Telisa said. "If there's no immediate response, come in after me. See what you can find. Take a peek in those buildings. We don't need to bring anything back, unless it's very easy."

Siobhan ack'd her again.

"Don't stay for longer than an hour this first time out," Telisa said. "I'll meet you back here. Once we have some idea what's going on, maybe we can try a longer stint next."

Siobhan nodded. "Understood." For the first time, Telisa believed Siobhan would be prudent. For some reason, that actually worried her, because it was a reminder that Siobhan and Caden were like her and Magnus had been.

Quit thinking like that. Magnus is alive. We'll be together again.

They each called in their two attendants and tucked them away in their small packs. Then they activated their stealth systems from the cover of the leaves. Telisa walked out. She saw Siobhan on her tactical, but Siobhan would not be able to see her. Telisa's alien cloaking sphere would not announce itself to Siobhan's link or her UNSF stealth suit. Siobhan turned off her directed tactical communications, so that she dropped off Telisa's view completely. They had decided full stealth was important, even though it would take a lot to detect the space force's DTC suite running on the suit.

Telisa actuated a mission timer. Cilreth had finally had a chance to learn how to recharge the cloaking sphere, so she had tested it to exhaustion. Under normal conditions with minimal movement, it had lasted for 29 hours. Telisa assumed if she remained active and generated a lot of noise that had to be dampened, that probably reduced the lifespan of the device.

The fence before them was more of a light net. No doubt it was strong. The hexagonal spaces looked like they would not quite allow a human head through.

It looks like a bird net, Telisa thought. *They were flyers, or what they needed to keep out was a flyer. Or did they just prefer to be able to see through the barrier? A human facility would have a wall if necessary, with optical sensors placed around the outside.*

The net rose 30 meters high between the towers. As they had seen from their observing attendants, the towers would deal with anything coming in from above that. Telisa had toyed with the idea of tunneling underneath the complex, but that would be a much more complex approach. If Shiny had still been on the team, they might well have done that. The Vovokan would be great at working underground since he had come from that environment on his homeworld.

She walked toward the fence and waited. Since Telisa had a tanto, her breaker claw, and a smart pistol, the plan called for Siobhan to cut the fence with her new laser pistol. Telisa smiled. Siobhan had happily turned in her 5-shot stunner for the laser pistol after they fled Sol. Imanol had looked on approvingly, calling the stunner a "core worlder weapon". He meant a weapon for civilized folk. It had been very painful to the flat alien body Telisa herself had inhabited, but otherwise the stunners were so carefully targeted to affect humans, and even then to a very limited degree, they were not likely to be effective against a random alien creature. Telisa doubted Shiny would be bothered by a stunner.

Siobhan started cutting. A section of the fence fell to the ground in a light breeze. Telisa moved forward quickly at first, covering a lot of ground. She ran over twenty meters onto the flat surface. She thought of the sensors on Skyhold that had noticed her weight.

Here's hoping the attendants didn't miss any surface sensors.

Telisa turned toward the buildings and waited. She did not see any response to her incursion or the damage to the net. She started to walk over to her side of the complex beyond. The open area was large. The closest building was over a hundred meters away.

Some movement caught her eye. It was one of the feeds from a scout machine spying from the forest where they had cut through. It saw a large machine approaching the net on low treads.

As I suspected. That vine-cutter is a multi-role machine. So Celaran.

Telisa felt encouraged that she had gained a feel for the alien race. Though so many things remained a mystery, she knew a thing or two about them.

Telisa loped toward the nearest building. She did not see any obvious entrances at the ground level. She approached closer to look for cracks in the surface that might indicate a flush door. She kept walking around the big building. A glance or two back the way she had come told her that the machine had started to repair the net with an unfamiliar tool. The tool was built into one of the arms, and the other arm ended in six long fingers, three on each side in opposition.

Six fingers. Like Celarans? Do Celarans even have fingers?

Some xenobiologists believed sophisticated manipulators were required in intelligent creatures. Something that did not manipulate its environment did not often need to be very smart. Telisa understood the idea, but she did not think it was an absolute. Probable, yes, but not a requirement.

The building had smooth walls around its perimeter, and the other buildings looked the same.

No doors around the sides. Just like the first tower building. They are flyers, they have to be. Or had to be.

Telisa turned her attention upwards. The buildings had complex roofs. She had spotted trap doors up there in the initial orbital scans. She referenced her link map of the place and found the nearest door visible from above.

She took a smart rope out of her pack. It remained within her stealth envelope, though when she used it, at least part of the rope would become visible. She gave the rope instructions, then threw it up with a lightning move.

The rope hurtled directly to the top of the wall before her, then a few seconds most of it dangled down. Telisa compressed herself, then launched upwards with a powerful contraction of her superhuman muscles.

She caught the rope and pulled herself up within another two seconds. Once at the top, she retracted the rope and hid it again. She moved to another spot on the roof and waited.

Something came to investigate. A black disc flew over to where the rope had been exposed. Telisa froze and watched it. She observed the turret on the top of the machine rotate. She saw an opening there, moving about and wondered what kind of weapon it was. Apparently it could be brought to bear on anything in the hemisphere above the top half of the machine by moving side to side as well as altering inclination.

I wonder if it can fly upside down.

Within ten seconds it gave up and flew away. The complex had noted an anomaly and sent a machine to investigate. Was it a smart AI ready to catch her next clue? Or just a dumb automaton that relied more upon firepower than brains? A Terran complex might have a central AI to control a squadron of guard machines. Telisa caught herself imagining this complex was controlled the same way.

Telisa decided the security machine might serve several functions like everything else the Celarans had made. She hoped that made it a mediocre combat machine at best.

She walked over to the nearest trap door and regarded it. Certainly whatever investigated the rope would take note of the door being used? Would it then set a trap for her? Telisa took the risk and slipped inside.

The building's interior was almost completely open. At first Telisa thought it was a cluttered hangar. Then she saw that work areas had been methodically placed throughout and separated by short walls of about waist height. The entire floor space was sectioned off into separate areas about as large as the *New Iridar*. She stood on a platform with no path down.

It's like one giant atrium! Makes sense. Flyers just use wide open space where Terrans would have hallways and stairs.

Telisa scanned the open platforms. Each platform had different types of machines. She saw one platform with an assembly that seemed to be making short towers only about 3 meters tall. Another cell had dozens of dodecahedral shapes stacked along its perimeter.

A factory maybe? Each area either stores, or creates, some different item. Time to steal something.

Telisa walked to the edge of the work area she had landed in. A series of silver and gold batons were affixed to the short wall around the edge of the space. She walked over and carefully released one from the wall. Her cloaking device decided it was part of her equipment and made it disappear. To Telisa, the stealthed item became ghostly, just as she saw her own arms and legs.

She had no idea what it was, but it was small, and light, so she slipped it into her pack.

Okay. I promised Siobhan just a look. Time to move on.

She took her prize back to the door. There, she looked took a second to look in all directions. She saw no signs of anything she could recognize as a threat. She saw something black hanging on a rod by the door. The rod was just like they had seen in the houses. Telisa looked closer. Some soft piece of black material hung there. It had silvery buttons or devices woven into it. Telisa saw black strings along an edge like laces or loose ties. She carefully lifted it from the rod and put it into her pack.

Telisa wondered what Celaran visual sensors looked like. Was something watching the door? Or did the door just report activity about opening and closing? Did it see everything that passed through? She pushed her way back out the door, ready for anything.

Back outside, she saw no sign of the flying discs she half expected. She moved away back to the edge and started to wonder if she could just jump back down. Then she saw three glider machines criss-crossing the grounds below.

Something's up. The machines know we're here. Time to get out.

Telisa hesitated. She decided even her amazing host body might break a leg dropping down from this height.

I could sacrifice the rope. Leave it behind as a distraction. The drawback being, I'd be leaving behind a clue as to who had come snooping around.

Telisa told the rope to drop her about five meters and then let go of the top. She took out her attendants as the rope hooked over the top of the building and wrapped around her waist. She hopped over the edge and told her attendants to dampen her fall.

The rope held her part of the way down, then it let go of the top and pulled itself back to her. She accelerated toward the flat lot below, though more slowly in the low gravity. Her attendants pushed hard against each of her hands, slowing her more. At the bottom, she landed and absorbed the impact well.

Telisa was congratulating herself on the agile landing when she looked up and saw one of the disks headed right for her. She simultaneously released the attendants and told them to defend her from close range. The disk rapidly closed. There was only one more second.

Telisa ducked.

The machine flew right over her and continued on, gaining speed. Telisa fumbled and brought out her breaker claw. She decided not to attack since the machine apparently did not see her.

145

It's headed toward Siobhan's area fast. Must be trouble.

Telisa saw another glider machine in the distance on a parallel course. Then another.

She needs my help.

Telisa moved quickly after the machine that had almost struck her, but as she considered the problem, she realized a distraction might be more valuable.

Maybe if I attacked one of the towers... damn, we should have arranged for a signal to make the others create an external distraction for us.

Telisa decided to follow the machines and see what had happened. She ran as fast as she could to keep up as they flew past one building and around another. Telisa considered dropping her cloak for just long enough to ask Imanol for a distraction. The alien machines were all around her. At least five of them would see her if she dropped her cover.

It would only take them a split second to react to me. I wouldn't make it if they wanted to shoot.

Something lay huddled on the ground just ahead. There was a dark spot. A pool of blood? Telisa's heart skipped a beat.

Telisa hurried forward. She saw the broken remains of one of the glider machines. There was a scorch mark on the artificial surfacing a meter from its slagged pieces.

Maybe it wasn't Siobhan, she told herself. *Maybe some wild animal got in. The electrical creature. No, that can't be it. They have her.*

Telisa ran from the spot in a wide circle, looking for more signs of struggle. Her imagination flashed images of pieces of Siobhan laying scattered on the ground, but reality produced no such horrors for her to find.

Nothing. She could have gotten away.

Telisa headed back to the rendezvous point. She was still worried. When Telisa arrived at the fence where they had entered, she saw the repair machine had finished its job and moved on. It did not surprise her. It had still been less than an hour.

Telisa waited. She brooded over whether she should be back searching or waiting, but most of the time had elapsed anyway. It would be worth waiting if Siobhan showed back up. When time ran out, Telisa cut through the fence with her super-sharp tanto and ran behind some of the largest vines at the edge. There, she uncloaked and checked her link.

Siobhan was not nearby. Telisa contacted Cilreth.

"Siobhan isn't back yet. Have you heard or seen anything?"

"No! Should we come help?" Cilreth asked.

"No, not until we make a different plan. I don't want to get anyone else shot or captured. I saw a destroyed guard machine, I think she must have had to kill it. I'm going back in to look for her. If she contacts you, tell her to stay outside the perimeter. I'll find her."

"And if you don't come back?"

"Then you're in charge."

"Cthulhu sleeps! You'd better come back."

Telisa cloaked herself and ran back inside. The repair machine had not yet been summoned.

First, that distraction.

Telisa took out a grenade and approached the nearest tower from inside the compound. Telisa told the grenade to go magnetic and detonate in ten seconds. The device clamped onto the surface of the tower. Telisa silently thanked the Five Entities that the tower had some ferrous material in its composition.

Telisa ran off deeper into the compound at her top augmented speed. She spotted the repair machine headed out. For good measure she rolled out a grenade targeted for it just as the first grenade exploded behind her.

Kaboom!

A second later, the next explosion destroyed the repair machine, sending its frame flipping through the air. It hurled away in a spectacular pyrotechnic display.

Kablam!

Wow. It wasn't as heavy as I would have expected.

Telisa selected one of the largest buildings in the area and ran for it as glider machines started to show up all over the complex. She thought of her smart rope as she ran, but she caught sight of a lower series of extensions to the building on one side. She ran toward the lower part of the building. As she neared it, she launched herself into the air with a powerful leap.

Seconds went by as she hurtled through the air. She asked for a small boost from her attendants and got it, delivering her onto one of the lowest roof surfaces. She landed off balance so she rolled with it. Her training and new agility paid off, allowing her to regain control of herself gracefully.

The exhilaration of the jump made her think of Siobhan.

She would have loved that. Please let her be in here.

Telisa glanced back at the smoke and debris she had left behind on the field. One large machine had emerged to clean up the mess, while the armored glider machines crisscrossed the field, searching for the enemy.

The roof was a gray-turquoise color. It slanted crazily in two or three different panes that adjoined the lower level she was on. Telisa climbed up like a spider, accenting her route with jumps as needed. At the top, she saw two doors and a collection of six windows in a long line.

If I break in, that would be more alarming to them, right? They will sense the door mechanism... but what choice do I have?

Telisa walked forward and hopped down onto the closest door. The portal opened under her weight and let her slip inside.

The interior of the huge building extended wide and open in all directions. Telisa landed on a small white platform that shook under her weight.

This is a launching platform. From here, I would glide where I need to go. It's for flyers, or for creatures that have some kind of flying assist.

Telisa thought over alternatives. Was her conclusion correct? She looked around at the huge space. To get here from below, she would have to be able to jump very well, glide, or fly.

They could have been merely gliders. Gliders turned flyers by technology. With boosters like my attendants, a light glider could get anywhere in here in a matter of seconds.

Did I make a flawed assumption? Maybe this building is purely robotic. Maybe real Celarans are not even supposed to go inside here. Then why does the door let me in? Why all the open space? Wouldn't machines make do with a denser work area?

And where the hell are they?

The building was filled with machines and equipment Telisa could not begin to understand. To her left was a series of enclosed cylinder tanks that looked like liquid or gas storage. To her right she saw five huge fabricators or power plants or... what? Pipes ran everywhere like a refinery or chemical plant. The space in the center of the building was oddly empty.

Clearly industrial... not a place to keep prisoners. I should search somewhere else...

A thin break line along the main floor caught her attention. The line cut right through the middle of the open area. Telisa caught sight of more seams in the floor to either side abutting the areas holding the machinery.

This is a big gateway in the floor!

Telisa glanced upward. Another giant crease along the ceiling made it clear the entire roof was meant to open to the sky.

Spacecraft hangar! I think... aircraft, at least? But Siobhan won't be here.

Telisa forced herself to stop looking for a way down deeper into the complex. Siobhan could be waiting outside due to a mix up, or she might be dead, lying on a table being dissected by Celarans. But if she had been captured and was still alive, Telisa had to find her and get her out.

She spotted a cylinder on one of the struts that supported her wobbly platform. She took a closer look. It was a separate piece. Telisa reached out and touched it. Nothing happened, so she grabbed it. The rod came away from the strut easily. She held it in her hand. It was about the same size and weight as the first rod she had taken in the other building. Telisa added it to her loot.

Telisa started to climb back out of the building. It would have been easier to send her smart rope ahead, but she did not want to give the Celaran security system any more glances of her equipment. Best to leave them unaware of her general position in case they had snatched Siobhan and were looking for another intruder to grab.

Telisa became aware of a saucer shaped glider approaching from her flank. She turned to watch it. The machine closed on her position, but its angle of approach was slightly off.

It knows I'm here, but it doesn't see me. That's what I get for using the door.

Telisa stopped. The machine slowed to a halt five meters from her. The top rotated one direction slowly while the wider bottom section spun the other direction quickly. It was odd to watch. She stared at the machine and thought of Siobhan.

If I get caught too, will that help or not?

Telisa compressed herself downward and told an attendant to go fly out over the main floor and record everything. She gave it an evasive course. The attendant flitted away, then the Celaran security machine launched itself after. Telisa jumped straight for the door with her hands forward like an upward dive. It let her through smoothly.

As soon as she emerged from the door, she saw three more of the gliders patrolling the roof of the building. They converged on her fast.

Okay, now they know I'm here.

Telisa leaped through the air to land on another facet of the roof. She ran up an angle of about twenty degrees, leaning into it. The machines peeled off after her.

And they can sense me! It's only a matter of time before they grab me, too.

Telisa took a sharp right and headed for the side of the building nearest the *New Iridar*. A flexuous machine appeared ahead. It had eight metallic tentacles arranged around a central hub that was smaller than her own torso. Each tentacle extended over three meters from the hub. The uncanny arrangement moved efficiently.

Not going to happen.

Telisa launched herself over the machine with a strong leap. The machine twitched as she passed overhead, confused. When Telisa landed on the far side, she kept running but dared a peek back. The machine had somehow re-acquired her.

Kerflump!

A bundle launched out of its midsection. Telisa turned sharply away, using her superhuman speed. Whatever the bundle was, it did not change course to pursue. She came to the edge of the building. The bundle fell away on her previous course. It opened into a net in mid-flight, covering the area she had been. It caught only air, then flipped over the side of the building.

151

First a net creature, now a net robot. Time to leave.

Telisa did not bother with the rope this time. She dropped straight off the edge. Instead of telling her attendants to lift against the gravity, she told them to push her toward the wall. In an instant she told her Veer suit to glove up her hands with her link. Her knees and hands scraped against the surface, slowing her fall. She grabbed at one ridge and then another as she passed them, slowing herself further.

She glanced upwards and saw two of the net launcher machines peering over the edge above her. The net that had been launched was floating back to the machine that had deployed it. The other machine was ready to fire at her.

Kerflump!

Telisa's lightning-fast reflexes were enough to give her time to push off from the side of the building before the net came hurtling down. She flew through thin air away from the building.

Now if I could only land without breaking my legs.

It seemed to happen slowly to Telisa's hyped nervous system. She told her attendants to thrust upwards as hard as they could. She rolled in the air before opening up her arms to increase her drag to land legs first.

An odd memory flashed through her brain of the first time Magnus had trained her to fall. He had made her fall over and over again in the simulation until her legs broke—

Smack!

The impact was manageable. She rolled with the impact, absorbing some of the energy in her legs as they bent, then the rest came through her Veer suit across her right shoulder as she rolled through it. Between the attendants, the Veer suit, her training, her augmented strength, and the lower gravity, Telisa was able to land, roll, and come up running in one smooth motion.

The VR stars got nothing on me.

Telisa ran in a zig zag pattern for the fence.

These are machines. If I let their guard go back down, then I can sneak back in and find her. Or maybe I can make a plan with the whole team.

Telisa decided against going back to the old rendezvous. She could check for Siobhan with her link once she made her way outside the compound. She took a left to skirt a building and find a new spot by the fence.

Vincent scuttled along the side of the building ahead.

By the Four.

The plant creature moved up to the side of the gray building and probed at the wall before it. Then it moved on. It did not seem to be moving urgently, though the creature was so alien it would be impossible to tell for sure.

Telisa felt angry at the alien for a moment. Was it working with the machines? Was it their ally? Or did the machines just leave things that looked like plants alone? Wouldn't a vine cutter come along and remove it?

How are you running around in here and what in R'lyeh are you doing?

She watched Vincent move along. One of the security gliders move by within forty meters of the alien. Vincent did not freeze, but neither did the glider pay it any attention.

Siobhan had better not be missing because of you, she thought grimly, then ran for the fence. As she approached, she launched herself onto it with one superhuman leap. She used her tanto to cut enough strands to let herself through, then retreated back into the vine jungle.

Michael McCloskey

Chapter 13

Telisa reappeared on Caden's link map. He waited the space of three nervous breaths. Siobhan did not appear. He strode back and forth atop the Celaran vine-spire that served as the lookout above their camp.

No.

Telisa moved toward base camp. Caden held himself from initiating a connection, just in case there was a valid reason for Siobhan's absence that was about to be announced. At the same time, his annoyance and fear rose.

Telisa should know we want a report right now!

"Why isn't she reporting?" Caden asked aloud. Beside him, Imanol had a look on his face that said it all: bad news.

"Is she talking to you?" Caden demanded.

"She's not dead, Caden. Captured. They captured her," Telisa reported.

"Who captured her, exactly?" he asked, struggling to stay calm.

They expect me to freak out. Fine. I won't. I'll stay calm and get her back.

"The security machines, as far as I know," Telisa said from the group link channel. "I have no reason to believe there are any Celarans. We went in, but turns out her stealth suit is not good enough. Whatever this stealth sphere is, it's a step up. I've been snooping around, but I don't know how to get her back yet."

"You can't find her?" Jason asked.

"No. A net casting machine came after me, so I think she's been netted and pulled into one of the buildings. The machines out there can't pinpoint me, but they know I'm around. I could probably go back in later and avoid detection for a time. That's one plan."

Telisa leaped up to their overlook and joined them. The ledge around the massive trunk was crowded, so

Telisa hopped over to a nearby vine. They heard rustling down below.

"Vincent is back," Imanol announced.

"Was Vincent inside the complex?" Jason asked.

"Yes," Telisa said. "Turns out he can wander around in there all he wants. He may be key to getting her back. If only we could really communicate with him."

"Then that's what we'll concentrate on," Caden said.

"I'm impressed. I expected you would be the first to demand we go in there guns blazing."

"We *are* going to go in there guns blazing, if we don't come up with something better," Cilreth said vehemently. Caden felt pleased to hear her express loyalty but he tried not to show it.

Telisa held up a black bag.

"I have some items. This race is most pointedly devoid of *stuff*. But maybe we can learn something from these knickknacks to help us get Siobhan back."

"Well we decided all their things have multiple functions," Caden said, thinking aloud. "So they don't need much stuff."

"As good a theory as any."

Telisa pulled something out. It was a black section of flexible material, with some kind of built-in shiny objects of various shapes and sizes.

"What the—" Cilreth said.

"Exactly," Telisa said. "I have no ideas here yet."

Caden examined the black material. Along one edge the black layer came together in thicker, denser cords like fasteners. It easily bent, stretched, and folded in his hands. He handed it to Cilreth, who stood eagerly by to get her own look.

Cilreth gave it a once over with some kind of scanner.

"It has a battery. That's all I've got," Cilreth said. "And it's damn complicated. Advanced."

Caden reached into Telisa's bag of loot and pulled another item out slowly. It was a cylinder about the length of Caden's forearm, though thinner. Caden took it in his hand. It felt incredibly light.

"Careful!" Jason urged. Imanol beamed like a proud father.

"That's a mystery too," Telisa said. She did not seemed worried about Caden's handling of the object.

"A simple club or structural beam?" Imanol suggested.

"I don't think so," Telisa said. "It's a complex powered device. I have another about the same size, but it's less complex, not powered."

"Wait. We have something going on out there," Imanol interrupted.

"What is it?" Telisa asked.

"One of those glider snakes just got taken down out of the air."

"Who cares? We need to concentrate on getting our team member back!" Caden said.

"What if the Celarans are coming after us out here?" Imanol asked. He brought his projectile pistol out.

"This could be something dangerous," Cilreth said. "I'm reviewing the footage. It wasn't a force tower pushing the glider away. Something *shot it down*."

"Siobhan?" Caden asked. He stood. He checked several visual feeds. He did not see his girlfriend, but something caught his eye.

The debris on the forest floor shifted. Then he saw it. A long brown monster scuttled over the surface. It was heavily camouflaged.

"We have visitors. On the ground," Caden said.

"Do they have guns?" asked Jason.

Caden frowned. The creature he watched was about the size and height of a young crocodile, perhaps three meters long. It had several stubby appendages that each split into three long spikes which sank into the detritus beneath it. Its head thinned into a snout that extended forward like the proboscis of a mosquito. The creature darted out of sight with surprising speed.

That thing is damn ugly. And dangerous, I bet!

"No guns I think," Imanol said. Apparently he had spotted it too. Caden saw one of their attendants go offline.

"It's attacking the attendants, too," Caden said.

"Grab your gear now! There's more than one. Several, at least," Telisa said.

Suddenly Jason's neck burned like fire. He yelled out in pain and slapped his neck. His hand came back covered in smoking blood. His Veer suit had gloved his hand before he could touch his own neck. Caden fell to his knees in shock.

"Caden!" Telisa said, dropping to his side. "Hang on. I'm checking your neck. Everyone take cover!"

Several things happened at once. Caden's suit told him it dropped painkillers into his blood and the pain faded to an ugly ache. His head throbbed with every heartbeat. The team brandished their weapons and dropped prone or to their knees. Imanol started to shoot his projectile pistol. Telisa poured water over Caden's head.

Is this it? Am I dead in the next few seconds?

Caden's suit extended to cover his head. The world blurred for a moment until his flexible faceplate hardened into a shape that provided no optical distortion.

"Acid," Telisa broadcast. "Those things are shooting wads of strong acid or base at us."

"I see them down on the ground," Jason said.

"My weapon is having a hard time deciding on the signature," Imanol rattled off quickly.

"I'm putting three attendants on it," Telisa said. "We'll have a signature within a minute. Just get going! Back to *New Iridar*!" Telisa told his suit to open at the neck. She took out a can of artificial skin and sprayed it across the back and sides of his neck. Then his suit sealed back up. Telisa pulled him upright.

Caden did not know if he could run in his muddled condition, but when he came to his feet, he felt good to go. Adrenaline and painkillers made for an odd couple in his system. He felt mentally calmed yet his heart beat hard in his chest. Telisa lingered beside him as he hustled down the vine they had arrived on. He asked the attendant for a course back and the machine provided it through his link.

I should be returning fire.

Caden reached for his sniper rifle.

"Wait until we have the signature. I want you to get ahead of us," Telisa said. "We'll cover you. Then you stop, take the sig, and cover us."

Caden focused on the route his link had brought up. He ran down another vine, hopped to an adjacent one, then ran through a hole in the giant leaves. He still felt like a tiny ant in a huge garden. An ant being pursued by a mantis.

"I'm hit!" Cilreth said on the channel. "My suit is holding for the moment!"

"It's burning through, let me pour some on there—"

"I'm hit too!" Jason said. "On my faceplate!"

Caden ran up to a complex vine junction. Directly before him sat Vincent. The Blackvine did not move. Caden let his hand rest on his stun/projectile combo pistol.

Is it making a move against me? No. Frozen in place. Great.

"Don't bother to help," Caden said aloud to the alien.

"What?" Telisa asked.

"Vincent is in my way."

He received a signature for the alien creatures advancing below. The target sig lacked precision. Apparently the things were so good at camouflage that the sig was hard to nail down. Or maybe they had a wide range of sizes and shapes. Despite Vincent's apparent lack of cooperation, Caden took a half second to convince himself the signature would not accept the Blackvine as a target.

Caden loaded it into his rifle. He leaped to one side, getting onto another vine. He saw droplets of blood fly as he landed. His own blood. It dribbled down his Veer suit.

So much for the fake skin. And there's a leak in my suit.

He pulled his rifle from his back and turned. He rested the rifle over the huge stem of a leaf and prepared to shoot. He realized a laser rifle would have been more useful in his situation, because it would have enabled him to carve out a longer shooting corridor through the leaves. He told one of the attendants flitting below to cut away some leaves ahead of him.

"Okay, I'll cover you from here," Caden said. "See if you can get around Vincent or just boot his ass to the ground."

Jason transmitted a nonverbal signal for distress.

"Got one but it got me too," Imanol said.

"Out of ammo," Telisa said. "Gimme your weapon."

Caden did not know who she was talking to. He focused on the feed from his rifle. The vines were dense and it was hard to see far, but he picked something up. He could tell from his tactical it was not a team member. Caden fired off two rounds.

Crack! Crack!

He would rely upon the signature to turn the rounds away if his target was something or someone unknown. It was risky, but his team was in trouble.

A round reported a strong hit probability on something matching the sig. Caden's suit fed him some noise from over on his right. An attendant reported another target, then it died. Caden shifted and fired off two more rounds.

Crack! Crack!

He got another hit report but three more possible targets showed up on his tactical. He took a deep breath. The attendant cutting leaves ahead of him darted forward, then dropped to the ground in a smoking spiral.

What if Siobhan's out there trying to get home with her cloak on?

Caden suppressed the thought. He would rely upon the rounds' ability to match the signature against the target. They were sophisticated. Besides merely veering away from non-matches, the rounds could even decide to stick together and inflict a through-and-through rather than disintegrate inside the target depending on a sig match or miss. Besides, the chances of accidentally hitting one Terran target in all that jungle were low.

Nice and calm. Take them out.

Caden started to fire more rapidly.

Crack! Crack! Crack!

"Way to go Caden! We're moving past your position," Telisa said. "I'll hang back beside you. Let's give the others some time to get ahead. Jason's leg is still injured from the other day."

Caden sent the nonverbal ack signal and fired again. The last attendant ahead of him dropped off the tactical.

"We lost our spotting. It's going to get dicey," he said. His effective range had just dropped below fifty meters. There were simply too many vines, spires, and leaves in the way without something ahead to sense the targets for him.

"They need another minute," Telisa said. "Wait. Or they don't! Fall back now, that's an order!"

Caden did not understand Telisa's mixed signals, but he picked up and retreated. His neck felt stiff. He did not dare touch it. Caden assumed the damage was causing inflammation despite the likelihood that his suit would try to counter it with drugs.

Caden walked down one vine at a slope, then stopped to climb up one of the artificial spires covered with smaller vines.

"Pick it up, Caden," Telisa said.

"I'll try—"

Caden was pulled up to the next vine in a second's time. He gasped in surprise, relieved to see it was only Telisa hauling him in.

"I never took you for the slow poke of the group," she said.

Caden ran across the next thick vine, then grabbed a leaf stem to keep from falling when it curved to the right. He could hear himself breathing inside the helmet. It sounded raspy.

A huge swath of forest erupted into bright light.

Vooosh.

Nuke!

Caden froze, waiting for his life to end. Instead, a wave of smoke rolled over him. His Veer faceplate did not let any smoke in, so instead of coughing he stared, helpless, as smoke roiled past his face.

"What the hell!" Imanol sent out.

"Keep moving toward the ship," Telisa said. "All we can do is hope that thing's targeting is good."

That thing? Of course. The battle sphere.

The smoke abated to the point that Caden could see a blackened section of leveled forest directly ahead. Then light came again. Caden cringed, but the light was farther away than the first one.

Hrm, those creatures probably won't stand in the open? So that's where I should be. Lightning never strikes twice.

Caden scrambled down his vine and ran out into the smoking ash-covered area, then he turned sharply right toward the ship. He kept his single remaining personal attendant close, just in case it was reporting his position to the battle sphere.

If it wants me dead, I'm dead either way. I think it wants those things dead.

Vooosh.

As if Caden's presence had been the only thing keeping the section of forest from destruction, as soon as he staggered out into the burned out area, the forest to his right flashed into a burning wall. His suit warned of breathing hazards, but Caden wasn't about to deactivate his faceplate anyway.

Caden stopped thinking and just struggled to make it to the *New Iridar*.

Vooosh.

Telisa found him and put her hand on his shoulder, slowing him.

"The battle sphere has us covered," she said. "Slow down. Head for our sick bay, what there is of it."

"How bad is it?"

"Your neck is burned badly. Deeply," Telisa said.

"I'll make it. Concentrate on Siobhan. Get her back."

"I will. Tell me about Vincent," she asked. "What did he do during the attack?"

"He did absolutely nothing," Caden said.

"Ah. Just froze, right? I think that's how they deal with stuff like this," Cilreth said.

"Doesn't seem very useful," Jason said.

"Well, if you look like a plant, acting like a plant isn't so bad. Who shoots at a plant?" Cilreth asked.

The battle sphere, Caden thought, but he did not say it aloud. He knew what she meant. *Oh. Did Vincent just get incinerated?*

"Well, yes, if you're on a planet where the plants aren't hunted by whatever is attacking," someone said.

Caden felt pain eating through the blocker his Veer suit had put into his bloodstream.

Great. All those raw nerve endings. I need more synthetic skin from my pack.

"Well, at least our watchdog proved useful," Cilreth said.

Telisa just stared at the battle sphere and said nothing. Caden felt woozy. He let them lead him to the ship.

Chapter 14

A scary machine with knobby metal limbs carried Siobhan inside a hexagonal weave net. Its body was small, incongruous with the length of its arms. Its eight limbs came together in a central juncture only about the size of her upper torso. Joints were set at four points along each of the arms or legs. The limbs were strong despite the thin rod composition. Siobhan could not overpower her captor. She had struggled at first, but it soon became clear waiting was her only option. She had been stripped of her weapons and equipment pack.

The machine brought her inside through a roof door and deposited her on a metal platform with rails around the sides. She gazed at the building beyond. The ceiling was much higher and larger than the platform, just as she had seen before she was captured. The wide open space immediately made her feel exposed and vulnerable.

Another of the creepy machines climbed onto the platform from below.

Are these Celaroid machines or just Celaran? If so, I don't want to see one of them. Pretty clearly not flying creatures if this is roughly what they look like. Just amazingly long arms.

The two machines worked to hoist Siobhan onto another smaller raised platform that could have been an oversized Terran coffee table. They gently set her down and then started to open the net. Grateful to be released, Siobhan pushed the net away from her toward one of the machines.

The machine surged forward, pinning her to the flat table with four segments of its legs. Siobhan screamed. She railed against the thin metal legs, but they were incredibly strong. She might as well have been struggling against solid rock. She was mostly immobilized at arms and legs. Another bar kept her head from rising more than a few centimeters.

What the hell is it doing!?

The machine froze. Her panic fled its course. Siobhan regained control of herself. She took a deep breath.

"It's just curiosity," she told herself. "They're just curious... not meaning to scare me."

Siobhan believed her words. She just said them out loud to calm herself against the panic of being trapped. The other machine moved up from the side and extended an arm. It came close to her face. Something soft ran over her cheek.

They won't dissect me. They won't. Fracksilvers, what if they ARE going to dissect me?

"I'm a sentient creature please don't dissect me!"

An arm came out from the other machine and tested the zipper of her Veer suit. The zipper wouldn't move unless her link told it to unlock, or she put her fingers on the surface in the manual release pattern she had set under her arm.

Clearly the machine had done some sort of mechanical scan, as it knew what the zipper was for. There was a tiny flash and a pinpoint of heat on her chest. The zipper broke.

Frackedpackets!

"No! Stay out of there!" she snarled. Once again Siobhan tested the arms. She tried to throw the machine off balance, but with such long limbs its base was too wide. She concluded it must be attached to the floor or the table somehow anyway.

An odd thought arose that caused fear to rise again: what if they were not aliens at all? What if she was just the toy of some Terran gang that had taken over the facility?

If I find out there are Terran men and women behind this, I'm going to be adding some new people to my kill list.

Her heart beat rapidly again. The arm slowed. It retreated.

Siobhan took deep breaths and struggled to relax again.

See? It slows when I get too agitated. It cares about my well being.

The arm returned and unzipped her suit about three centimeters. Siobhan bristled. It was all some kind of nightmare. She found herself wishing it was virtual for no sensible reason. Virtual torture somehow seemed cleaner and less personal.

The machine folded over a bit of her suit at the zipper. The end of its limb hovered over the exposed skin for a moment, then swabbed it with something soft. Then it let go of the suit and pulled the zipper back.

Siobhan took another deep breath and counted her lucky stars.

Aliens. Aliens. Just curious and see? They can tell I don't like that.

"Thanks," she muttered. Then, a little louder, she said, "Let me go please?"

There was a loud clack from somewhere nearby. It put her nerves on edge yet again. The other machine had grabbed a long tool. It came toward her.

"I'm sorry I trespassed," she said in desperation. "Can you understand me? Do you even speak?"

The tubelike tool stopped over her head, then slowly moved downwards.

It must be scanning my insides. Or irradiating me to see if that kills me.

The arm pointed its tool lower, heading down her torso. Then it moved over her left leg. It hummed and paused again. Siobhan's neck hurt to stare down so sharply in her restricted position, but she was too scared to not watch. A huge needle snapped out of the tool.

167

"Fracksilvers!" she yelled in combined fear and anger. She struggled anew, then the needle met her suit. The Veer skinsuit reported dangerous surface pressure at a tiny point on her leg. Then she felt the prick as the suit reported a very tiny failure point. She forced herself to be still. It did not hurt much.

Is it injecting or sampling? Sampling. They are just sampling. Please just be sampling.

Siobhan's heart redoubled its pace. She struggled for breath. The arm retreated.

"I guess it's nice you stop when I get scared, but now I get the feeling you're just pausing and plan to continue anyway."

To her own ears, her voice did not sound as careless as she had been shooting for. She listened for a moment. The hangar was big, mostly quiet. There was a background hum. The air felt fresh and at a comfortable temperature on her face, though it was hard to tell. Her skinsuit regulated her temperature and aided in evaporation of sweat in the heat as well as closing off to add insulation for colder climes.

The arm moved forward again. She tensed. It stopped above her face.

"Careful! Now think about what you're doing there—"

A series of lights flashed into her face. She squinted. Then the light became dimmer. She opened her eyes a bit more. She saw a black pane hovering before her eyes.

It's testing my vision.

The black pane showed a single horizontal white line across the top. Then the line descended. She tracked it. Then two parallel lines descended together. Then three. Then four.

"Yes, I can count, thanks," Siobhan said, though she calmed considerably. This was certainly much better than being scanned and poked.

The single line descended again. Siobhan had a sudden inspiration.

"One!" she said. She synced up with the lines as they descended. "Two... Three.... Four."

The sequence repeated itself so she did too.

Two lines ascended from below and two lines from above. They met in the center, then descended.

"Two plus two equals four," she said. More lines met in the center. Each time she described the sequence aloud. Then lines formed in the center and subsets of them descended leaving lines behind, so she started to speak out the subtraction involved. The intuitive sequences continued for multiplication and division.

This seems reasonable. They think kind of like us, maybe.

Soon her link started to report noise. She suppressed the warning. Siobhan knew her link queried for service lists several times per second. No doubt the Celaran investigation had turned up its requests on the link frequencies.

"Can I talk to whoever's in charge here? Well, actually, anyone at all?"

Abruptly the rods securing her against the platform rose. The machine retreated a meter then stopped.

A floating platform smoothly joined the platform she stood on. The low wall around the area opened to allow access to the mobile platform. Lights blinked insistently at her from the contrivance.

"You want me to go that way," Siobhan said aloud. She took a nervous breath.

I can't believe I made it through that. I think they are going to let me live, maybe even let me go! Or they just want to get my hopes up. If they kill me now I'm really going to be pissed.

Michael McCloskey

Chapter 15

The forest around them was a ruined mess of incinerated debris. Telisa was reminded of the destructive capability of the Vovokan battle sphere. Thanks to Momma Veer, Caden's rifle, and the sphere, the entire team had survived the sudden attack.

At least this time our watchdog played the role of bodyguard, she thought.

Imanol summed it up out loud. "Well, Shiny's pet made short work of them." Imanol had been hit by the caustic substance, but required minimal first aid since his suit had taken most of it. Jason's faceplate was ruined and his face was red but mostly unburned. Cilreth had burns on one leg and another partially ruined combat suit.

We're under equipped, Telisa thought. *Before, we would have had all the replacements we could want. Now... every ruined suit is going to be missed.*

"It's too bad, those things were nothing but wild animals. They didn't deserve that," Cilreth said.

"You handled it well," Telisa sent her privately.

"Thanks, but I turned on the emotion stabilizer at the first sign of trouble," Cilreth said back on their channel.

"That's fine. It worked."

"We have a right to defend ourselves," Imanol said in response to Cilreth's original thought.

"By incinerating every last one of them?"

"We didn't. The sphere did. I would have been satisfied to shoot a few up front and run—"

"You can debate that later. We have to concentrate on Siobhan right now," Caden said.

"I agree, Caden. This little fight gave me an idea. It's time we introduced the Celarans to our spherical friend," Telisa said.

"Wait a second," Cilreth said on the group channel. "Are we starting a war with an alien race?"

She's right to hesitate. But I'm making this call.

"They have one of our people," Telisa said. "Besides, there are no Celarans here, just automated defenses. That's pretty clear from the empty settlement. With all the snooping around we've done on this planet, if there were a couple left, they'd be aware of our presence by now. I think a guard robot took Siobhan and incarcerated her. If it's a real Celaran that took her, they deserve a hostile response."

Even as Telisa said it, she knew she was making some assumptions. Maybe there was only one Celaran on any given planet and it lived in there. Maybe the Celarans were only robotic now, having discarded their old bodies. Maybe to Celarans, trespassing was a killing offense. Any number of possibilities could explain everything, and they did not all work well with her plan. Yet she felt she had to act.

There's one more advantage to this. If our watchdog is destroyed, all the better.

"It could kill her," Caden said. His voice was different, softer, despite his determination.

His suit has him on painkillers. But it would be no use to order him to rest now. It would just be torture for him.

"We have to get her back. Let's get started," Telisa said aloud.

"Everyone in the ship," Telisa broadcast through her link. "We're landing just outside the perimeter of the third site."

"I want to hurry," she said switching back to speaking aloud. "Let's give the watchdog minimal time to recharge."

"The force towers—" Cilreth started.

"Are designed to keep out wildlife, not spacecraft," Telisa said. "What good would it do to push a spacecraft away? Most ships have long range weapons systems."

172

"Okay, though you warn us about such assumptions," Cilreth said.

"We'll drop from the sky right onto the base and let our Vovokan friend loose. If some of you want to hoof it over there, I guess you don't have to come with me. The ship will be a target."

"Wait. If *New Iridar* is heavily damaged, we might never get back," Imanol protested.

"We have to get Siobhan back," Telisa said.

"There's a middle option," Cilreth said. "We can land just outside the edge. It might keep the ship from being a target to the automated defenses. But we know the battle sphere will come out to patrol the vicinity..."

"And it will see the Celaran machines as a threat. And vice-versa, when it starts to incinerate the perimeter net or a tower or a patrolling robot," Telisa finished.

"If we have to, we can take a shot or two to get things started," Caden said.

"We can try just outside the perimeter. It makes sense," Telisa said. "The *New Iridar* is valuable. If it's destroyed, I don't know if we would survive. I'm not sure we can digest that sap or any of the life here."

"Honestly, which side do you think will win?" Imanol asked.

She turned to look at Imanol. "I have no idea which side will win. Part of me wants to go looking for Siobhan during the battle, but I guess I'll wait until there's been some damage to the Celaran guard machines. I'll also have a better chance without having to worry about being killed by stray fire."

The others loaded up into the Vovokan shuttle. Cilreth told the *New Iridar* to prepare for takeoff. The battle sphere took the cue and entered the ship as Telisa did. They prepared for flight inside the small ship.

Telisa brought up the satellite maps of the third site as she secured herself in the sleep web of her tiny quarters.

She pushed down a pang of loneliness that came to assail her. Her sleep web had been so warm and happy with Magnus around. She remembered their giant bedrooms on the *Clacker*.

"There," she said, passing Cilreth the target spot. It was fifty meters from the edge of the Celaran hardtop. "Everyone, fan out along the perimeter when we get there. Take cover behind some heavy vines. Caden and I will light the fire, if it's necessary."

"Okay, give me ten minutes to get us there," Cilreth said.

"Got it," Caden said.

The others provided nonverbal acks.

"Hang with me, guys," Telisa said. "I would give you more time to recover from your injuries, but I don't want us *all* to have time to recuperate."

Telisa did not know how long it would take for the Vovokan battle sphere to restore its energy reserves, but she hoped it would not be ready to face the Celaran machines. The sphere seemed stronger than anything she had seen from the Celarans yet, though it was hard to gauge the relative power of such disparate forces.

Cilreth brought the *New Iridar* in just over the massive alien spires and huge leaves. That suited Telisa just fine, since she was not completely sure the towers could not hurt their craft. They approached the compound without incident. The ship slowed, then settled back down amid the spires, crushing vines and debris underneath it as it settled. The towers were quiet.

As expected, the system is smart enough to know the difference between a few wild flyers and a spacecraft.

Everyone headed for the exit ramp. The team dispersed along the fence. Telisa winced, seeing people limping out with holes in their suits. The Vovokan sphere floated out and headed straight for the Celaran installation.

By the Five, it's about to go crazy out here.

"Cover," she reminded everyone. Telisa took up a spot near the ship. The team all knew enough to stay out of the open, but when Telisa got worried she reminded them anyway. Caden stayed nearby, waiting for her order.

"Shoot at one of the towers," she told him. "I'll go in and stir something up."

"Careful," he said. She looked at him, but he was already lining up a shot with his sniper rifle's software.

Caden took a couple of shots. A round of counterfire came in immediately.

Crack. Crack. Ka-ching!

An attendant exploded in front of them as incoming fire hit it. Caden stopped shooting and stepped behind a trunk.

"That should do it," Telisa said. She activated her stealth sphere and approached the outer fence.

The return fire from Celaran machines within the base galvanized the battle sphere to action. It launched its own assault against the nearest tower.

Kzap, kzap, kzap.

Telisa did not know if Caden's incitement had been necessary, but in any case the battle had begun. The Celaran tower was slagged in seconds, bringing down the fence nearby. Telisa saw more Celaran disks coming out of the buildings to engage.

Kting. Crack. Crack. Bzing.

The disk machines shot projectiles at the sphere but its powerful shields shrugged the fire off. Telisa saw evidence of some energy weapons being used, causing a shimmering in the air. Her attendants and link picked up noise at frequencies above visible light.

Telisa ran through the open section of fence and headed along the inside perimeter. She was about thirty meters from the battle sphere. Her link showed her breaker claw ready. She felt the alien weapon could destroy the battle sphere if its shields were brought down. Did it know where she was? Failure could bring fatal retaliation.

Maybe if I wait until the shields are absorbing fire... if the Celarans have enough left to give me an opening.

Telisa did not have to wait long. Another group of gliders moved in from her left and concentrated their fire on the Vovokan machine. She saw the battle sphere's shields flicker.

Now!

Telisa activated her breaker claw on the battle sphere.

Kraaazap! Thwack thwack thwack.

The shields held. The sphere struck back at the Celarans. Five or six of the security machines became flying heaps of slag that disintegrated in the air. Smoking parts rolled across the hard flat surface of the lot surrounding the buildings. Smoke started to obscure most of the complex before them.

"Five help us," she muttered.

At least it didn't hit me back.

Telisa increased her distance. She wondered if she should go look for Siobhan but she decided to stick to the plan. Was the Vovokan battle sphere going to destroy the entire base? Would Siobhan get hurt wherever they had her held?

"Telisa—" Caden said on their channel.

"Blood and souls!" exclaimed Imanol.

Okay, I'm missing something...

Telisa looked up. Above the largest building, a long, flat shape hovered. Telisa realized it was the building where she had seen the doors in the floor and ceiling.

Of course. The spacecraft! It's real enough.

The Vovokan sphere saw it too. The machine lanced out with energy weapons.

Kraaazap zrap zrap!

They had no effect. The hovering ship flickered as it unleashed *something.*

176

The battle sphere's shields failed and the machine dropped. It struck the ground. Several holes appeared on its surface, emitting sparks and smoke.

Back off—

KABOOM!

The machine exploded across the field of pavement. Telisa was hurled back and landed roughly on the hard surface several meters away from where she had been standing.

"We did it!" Caden transmitted. "Telisa, did you see that?"

"Telisa?"

"Where is she?"

"Wait! I can see her! She's hurt!" Imanol said.

"What?" Telisa mumbled, stunned. She lifted her head and saw her body lying on the ground in plain sight.

"Come with me!" Caden said.

"Caden!"

"He's right! Go in!"

Telisa went to sleep.

Michael McCloskey

Chapter 16

Huornillel retreated from the Celaran stronghold when it was clear the new creatures were not making constructive progress. They were in fact much worse off than she was, having to hide like vermin on the base since their race did not have any exposure to Celaran civilization. The guardian machines did not recognize them as friend or foe.

Huornillel enjoyed a straightforward mutual avoidance relationship with living Celarans, but her relationship with their guardian machines was much more complicated. It was a crazy mixture of dominance-avoidance with some of their static tools, where she enjoyed dominance, but the living-tools, the machines that emulated life, those operated on mutual avoidance unless Huornillel tried to go to the restricted spaces. Then everything fell apart and it became a confrontation relationship.

Aliens. They are all totally crazy.

'Contextual interrelational reaction', she called it. Some of the primitive creatures on her homeworld operated on these principles: in some situations they would choose avoidance, in others, confrontation, in yet others they could coexist in dominance-avoidance pairs. Anything was possible and it could shift at any time. It was exactly why wild animals were considered dangerous. They were unpredictable. Wild animals, and aliens.

Her toolkit observed something interesting from a Celaran interface she had studied and learned about. One of the alien visitors had been dropped off in the vine forest. It was alone.

These others still operate in coordinated fashion. Therefore, the lone one is not the dominant one, provided it is isolated as I suspect.

Could Huornillel intercept the lone one and establish a dominant relationship? Then that alien would become part of her network. If only she had been able to break their control protocols. That was proving very elusive. Still, it might be worth a try, she decided.

Huornillel had been marooned on this planet for so long. What else did she have to do?

***

Siobhan stood unsteadily on a vine and listened to the sounds of the alien forest. Her hands shook. She wondered if she had been drugged or if she suffered tremors from the ordeal. Even though she usually thrived on danger, she was not used to anything like she had gone through in the Celaran building. At some point after entering a new platform her memory ended. Then she had regained consciousness back in the forest, alone.

"Telisa? Telisa can you hear me?"

Siobhan tried to open a channel to Telisa but it did not work. If Telisa had been captured and released as she had been, the Celaran robots must have let the other PIT member loose somewhere far from here. She tried to remember the range of a civilian link without public boosters. She did not think it was far. Less than a kilometer, maybe.

Siobhan had her weapons and her pack. They had given her the tools she needed to survive, at least, though her stealth suit was dead. Totally out of power. She figured they did not want her to disappear on them again. Her hand went to her front zipper. They had started to take the suit off, then stopped. If she remembered correctly. They *had* stopped, hadn't they?

The vine forest had not been as intimidating before, when Siobhan had attendants and teammates all around her. Now, her link saw no services except those offered by her own equipment and weapons. She had no video feeds of what was going on around her.

There could be something stalking me right now, and I wouldn't know it.

Siobhan glanced behind her at the thought. She wished she could activate her stealth suit.

I don't know how long I'll be out here on my own. I need to be careful. Which direction should I go?

She stared up at the system star overhead, shining between two massive leaves. Her link returned her approximate location based on the time of day and the angle of the star. The answer hurt. She could be as far as 25 kilometers from the last position of the *New Iridar*.

Siobhan turned west toward the ship and started to walk. She held her laser pistol in her hand and her shock baton hung from her belt. She thought about the dangers they had encountered so far.

Net creatures and bulbous silver things with tentacles. Wonderful.

It got rougher. Siobhan felt drained of energy herself. Without an attendant to map a good way, she often found herself stuck out on the ever-shrinking end of a vine, or walking on a large one that twisted back the way she had come. At least with her link working, she would not get lost, even though there was nothing to connect to outside of her own tools. She stopped and drank some water. She had enough to last her the journey, provided she got home in good time.

Does it ever rain in this awful place? I wonder if I can drink the sap of these things like those bat-creatures.

A shot rang out through the forest. Then another. Siobhan dropped onto the waist-thick vine she was on and hugged it with her arms.

Who's shooting at me!?

Siobhan did not see anything, but she heard something out in the forest. A crackling sound. It sounded almost like fire. She looked into the sky for signs of smoke. She did not see any from her positions.

She aimed laser pistol back eastward and waited, prone atop the thick vine. Something came into view.

The creature looked like a huge army ant. Except instead of an ant's head, the foremost body part was dominated by a circular opening. Two wide black orbs sat on either side of the tube. Huge eyes? The thing had no mandibles or teeth.

Then she saw another. And another. Within another ten seconds she saw seven altogether.

My packets are fragged.

Without moving a muscle, Siobhan let her pistol take a target signature from the creatures. She prepared it to fire on them but waited.

Fight... run... or just sit here and don't move.

Siobhan told her stealth suit to activate in vain. It did not comply. She rose onto her knees and elbows, preparing to retreat.

Kablam!

The vine exploded in front of her. The next second she was hurtling downwards.

Siobhan found herself lying on her back in a rotting pile of giant leaves. Her pistol was not in her hand. She grabbed her shock baton, trying to clear her head. She felt fear and confusion.

Calm. Think. I have grenades.

Siobhan talked to a grenade with her link and gave it the signature she had collected. It detached and moved ahead slowly. Siobhan did not give it the signal to attack.

She heard the things coming. Siobhan's stealth suit reported a new malfunction. One of its main processors had shut down, reducing its responsiveness to attack.

So this is how I die. Equipment damaged from explosion. No power for stealth. Surrounded by alien critters. How the hell do those things shoot? That huge opening in their heads? Insane.

For some reason she thought of sea divers who died in underwater caves when their flashlights all failed to operate.

The first creature walked into sight. Another one came behind it. Though headed in her general direction, they did not seem to be coming right at her. The things were looking up into the trees.

Is there something else up there?

The creatures were each the size of a dog. She saw now that the things had long whiskers that barely touched the leaves and roots below them.

They don't see me. Now is a good time to use the grenade. But last time I moved it did not go well.

Siobhan told the grenade to stand by. She lay frozen, waiting.

As she watched, one of the creatures became agitated. But it was not at her. The thing was still looking *up*.

Bang!

Then the creature's head exploded in sparks and smoke. The thing dropped dead, smoke pouring from the gaping orifice in its head.

That thing just... launched a projectile and died.

Siobhan suddenly thought she understood the thing. Like a bee willing to sting and die, this thing shot its mini-cannon and died in the act.

So it brings down food from above. Flyers, too. Ah, but that means... something is coming to eat me.

She had been "shot down" like a bird. Now she was chow lying on the forest floor waiting to be collected! Siobhan had another, even more dreadful thought.

Only two grenades... should I save the last grenade for myself? Or can I kill myself with a shock baton? I can't believe I traveled all this way and it comes to this. Caden! If I don't make it I'll never see him again.

She accessed the baton's documentation with her link and read through the warnings while the ground shooters walked by her. None of them seemed to target her again. They all were looking upwards, scanning for things to shoot. Siobhan concluded the baton could not kill her directly with its charge. Of course, if she could bash her own brains in with it, there was always that.

Siobhan shed her defeatist line of thought and prepared to defend herself. She tried to stand. Her arms and legs were functioning thanks to the amazing protection of the suit, but it was hard to walk on the surface. She wobbled upright. Rotted leaves covered the area. Wherever she stepped, her foot broke through and slid into empty space below, filled only with mush or air pockets between the roots.

Fine, I'll roll, or crawl, or something. I can't climb upwards without being shot again.

Siobhan crashed through the forest. Each time her leg pushed through the surface detritus and sank deep in, she half expected some sub-surface monster to grab hold of it. She knew the Veer suit was tough. That helped calm her. Her usual fearless demeanor had been shaken.

Siobhan made it past three spires before she saw the next creature. She knew instantly, this new thing was exactly what came after the shooters to clean up the fallen food. It looked like an armored pig with ant-legs and a wide set of mandibles. Hundreds of colorful sensor-hairs fanned out around its "mouth" that made it look like a terrifying combination of a tusked boar, an armadillo, and a peacock.

Now or never. Climb or grenade or baton or die.

She looked for the shooters. She could not see any. Siobhan knew if she started to climb, chances would go up that one could spot her above.

She told her grenade to take it out. The device hurled forward. It followed a vine and made good progress at first, then it slipped off the side and fell into the bed of detritus. Siobhan heard the tiny click of its digger spines coming out. Then the grenade struggled to make its way forward. It became visible again, made it another meter, then fell into the mass of leaves and vines and roots again.

The grenade was still closer than she wanted it, but she knew it had good directional blast control, and she had her suit. She would only have to cover her face, or at least look away. The alien seemed to detect her. It moved for her, allowing the grenade to intercept.

Ka-Boom!

The thing exploded into pieces which rose, struck the leaves above, then rained back down. It was filled with purple fluid that dripped from the leaves and vines all around. As the detonation sound faded from her sonic-dampener-protected ears, Siobhan heard a new scuttling in the forest. The blast had agitated something. A lot of somethings.

Please be running away...

Two more of the awful scavenger things crawled into view. She thought she heard at least one more. They crawled toward her.

Jammers. That was a mistake.

More adrenaline poured into Siobhan's system. She came alive. She found solid footing on a large root below the debris underfoot and held the baton ready. The first creature arrived. Its long sensor hairs brushed over the leaf nearest her. She held out the shock baton.

"Back it!" she barked.

The sensor hairs brushed the baton. The creature recoiled. It emitted a loud squawk that caused yet another adrenal burst in Siobhan.

Then it charged.

Siobhan only had time to shove the baton between the stubby things she assumed were mandibles. The baton reported a full discharge. The thing below her squawked again and thrashed.

"Frackjammers!" she yelled. The other two things were coming quickly now.

Siobhan brought up the shock baton and slammed it down onto her attacker. It sank in with a wet crunch. She saw more of the purple blood. She kicked the corpse back savagely, blocking the line of attack of another armored pig.

The third darted in and grabbed her ankle in its jaws.

The Veer suit distributed the bite well, but Siobhan felt significant pressure on her lower leg. It was just enough to creep her out but not enough to seriously hurt her leg. The baton crashed down again and delivered another shock charge. Her Veer suit insulated her from any of the current that might have traveled through her.

The jaws refused to come off her ankle, though the scavenger beast stopped moving and leaked prodigious amounts of the bright ichor. Siobhan squared off against the third, though her right foot was hard to move with its extra load. This time, she had a nice clear swing, so she let go with her full strength. The crunching sound came loud and wet. The thing toppled aside next to its brothers, unmoving.

Siobhan stood unsteadily, already breathing hard. Two more armored creatures walked around stalks and trunks into sight. Siobhan felt something on her ankle. She looked down. The remains of the thing attached to her leg was still trying to bite her. She noted with horror that even the first creature, which she assumed dead, had started to wriggle anew.

"Hard to kill huh? *Oh I will* kill you," she rasped. Another creature came into sight, bringing her total unharmed enemy count to three. She breathed heavily and wiped the gore off her shock baton. This time two of them would arrive at the same time from opposite directions. To avoid this, Siobhan stepped toward one, dragging her right foot with effort. Her left foot fell through the undergrowth, bringing her face to face with the thing coming.

"Arrrgh!" she yelled in disgust. The creature came into range, clacking. Its limbs and hairs were disgusting. A rich scent assailed her. Siobhan attacked all out, afraid the other would arrive from behind too soon. She thrust the baton into its maw. That stopped its forward march. Then she anticipated its angry charge and met it with an even stronger thrust. The baton cracked against its hard exterior and caused purple mush to ooze out.

Siobhan heard the other one close behind her and panicked. She pressed the baton down onto the bug before her, supporting herself, and climbed right over it. She almost screamed in frustration at the one clinging to her ankle.

One free second and I swear I'm gonna smash that jammer off my leg so damn hard!

Some part of her realized she was making gasping mewing sounds that did not at all sound as ferocious as she would like. She pivoted on the last foe and brought the baton down savagely on the one that had threatened to get her from behind. This time the wet crack was expected. It was spectacular, sending purple goo flying. She smashed it again and again.

Another two pig-things came forward. They had to run the gauntlet of corpses surrounding her, but she knew they would make it to her. She pried most of the body off the pair of mandibles that stubbornly clung to her leg. That one still struggled despite the mess of its body, but without a pair of jaws, she counted it out of action.

Her last grenade was ready to blow up if it looked unwinnable. Siobhan struggled for breath. The smell felt like it was suffocating her now.

I can take one more with me. Always one more. Just kill the next one then I can die.

Siobhan heard a rattling sound like an angry snake.

What now? Another creature come to fight for a meal?

The scavenger pig before her started to thrash in anger or distress. Then it slowed and froze. Siobhan looked over her shoulder at the new danger.

It was Vincent.

"Vincent?" she said uncertainly. "Are you helping me?"

The Blackvine did not answer. It shuffled over. Siobhan's link picked up noise. Ironically, Siobhan suddenly felt creeped out by the alien. She told herself it was crazy. It had just saved her from monsters trying to eat her.

Why does the quiet plant freak me out? Because I'm a mess. Fragged.

Siobhan pried herself up. She was tired, very tired. She did not think she could climb back up into the vines. Besides, what if there were still more of the shooter ants or pigs around?

"What now?" she asked.

Vincent's link sent her a nonverbal command.

"Prepare."

Siobhan rose unsteadily. She looked around.

"Repair."

Vincent held out her laser pistol. Siobhan took it.

"It's fine, according it its diagnostics," she said. She re-armed it and kept it in her hand, searching for enemies.

Vincent sent more of the nonverbal codes. *"Repair. Return."*

"What?" She sent the nonverbal command for lack of understanding.

Vincent sent a tendril out. The alien wrapped the tendril around her pistol.

"Return."

"You want it?" Siobhan felt torn. Vincent had just saved her life. Now it wanted something very useful back.

Vincent pulled the pistol from her hand, but held it between them.

"Authorize."

Oh. It won't listen to his link. That's why he asked me to 'repair' it.

Siobhan felt nervous. She decided to help, since she still had her baton. Some paranoid part of her prepared to duck and swing the baton at Vincent if for some inexplicable reason the alien decided to shoot her with her own pistol after saving her. As soon as the thought crossed her brain she realized she could easily prevent that from happening.

Siobhan accessed the pistol through its link interface. She verified the pistol had her on its no-target lists, then authorized Vincent to use the weapon, while keeping herself as the owner. Vincent would not be able to convince the pistol to shoot her. She gave him permission to inquire status, arm, fire, and add new target profiles.

That should do it. Unless he's as good a hacker as Shiny is.

Apparently, Vincent saw the new services appear in his link. He targeted one of the dead bodies before them and fired. Smoke rose from the disgusting purple mass.

"Satisfied?" Siobhan asked.

"Follow."

Vincent headed west toward the New Iridar. Siobhan shrugged to herself and followed.

Michael McCloskey

Chapter 17

Jason ran across the hardtop toward Telisa. He had not given it a moment's thought; it was his instant reaction to seeing her drop. Caden was at his side, then outpacing him.

"Wait for cover fire!" Imanol yelled. Jason's tactical showed two grenades rolling away from Imanol's position.

Blam, blam. Blam, blam.

"No, cease fire!" Cilreth said. "Let them think the enemy was the battle sphere. Otherwise that ship will destroy us next."

Jason did not see or hear the grenades explode. He assumed that Imanol had disarmed them as Cilreth suggested. Jason focused on reaching Telisa quickly. Caden reached Telisa and grabbed one of her arms. Jason grabbed Telisa's other arm and dragged her with Caden. They seemed to move so very slowly while the reports of projectile fire echoed around the field.

We can make it out, Jason said to himself, though he feared otherwise.

Jason looked at Telisa. There was blood on her face. He could not see any holes in her Veer suit, but he knew if it had been penetrated it might reseal and staunch her bleeding. His link checked with her suit. The suit said its occupant was still alive.

"She's only stunned," Jason said hopefully.

"Who? Where is everybody?"

Jason was confused for a full second. That female voice... his link identified the speaker as Siobhan.

"Siobhan!" exclaimed Caden. "Where are you? My tactical shows you approaching the *New Iridar* from the forest!"

"Yep, I'm here," Siobhan said. "I see smoke. The ship isn't hit is it? Who are we fighting?"

"The ship? Ask how many times I've been hit!" Caden said, holding his head low and pulling Telisa toward the forest.

"I'm there in a couple minutes!" Siobhan said.

"Meet us at the *New Iridar* or beyond. The battle sphere is gone," Imanol told her.

The PIT team ran into the vines of the forest. The battle died down behind them. No projectiles or energy beams cut into the forest from the compound.

If that Celaran ship goes for the New Iridar, we'll be stuck here forever, or close to forever.

Caden and Jason stopped to rest about fifteen meters outside the fence. They placed Telisa with her back to a huge vine spire.

"That was a disaster," Imanol said.

"We got rid of the battle sphere," Telisa mumbled.

"You're back! Take it easy," Jason said.

"Temporary brain scramble," Telisa said. "Luckily I'm only a copy," she said, managing a slight smile.

"Siobhan is back," Caden told her, already loping off toward the *New Iridar*.

"Follow him," Telisa ordered, though she did not move.

Jason started to prop her up. "No hurry, I think," he said. "The Celarans aren't pursuing us."

"I think they're smarter than we give them credit for," Cilreth said. "They know we're not violent."

"Well, at least they're peaceful," Telisa said. "They only defend themselves if attacked."

Telisa stood. Jason hovered nearby, ready to help.

She's probably recovered. And once again, several times stronger than me, Jason thought.

"Catch up with Caden," she said, moving forward. Jason could tell she was not one hundred percent because she did not use her amazing strength to leap up to a wider vine above.

"Tall order. Wunderkind wants his girlfriend back," Imanol said. But he ran up the vine and tried to catch Caden.

By the time Jason and Telisa arrived, Caden stood below the *New Iridar*.

Jason checked the map. It showed Siobhan and Vincent were almost there.

"Be careful," Jason said. "This could be a deception."

"Hey! The green recruit is paranoid!" Imanol said proudly.

"He's not green anymore," Telisa said, readying her weapon. "Like he says. Stay sharp."

Jason walked over and took partial cover at the base of a vine. There were no attendants for him to command, but a Terran scout machine lingered near the *New Iridar*. He added its video feed to his attention cycle. The view flipped into his PV rotation periodically.

Siobhan emerged from the forest with Vincent beside her.

Caden loped forward and embraced her.

"I thought you were a goner for sure," Caden mumbled against her. Siobhan simply clung to him tighter.

Jason glanced at Imanol, but his acerbic companion did not say anything. He looked pleased.

"Vincent found me at a critical moment. Maybe saved my life."

"I take back everything I said about him," Imanol said. *Maybe Imanol is human after all.*

"Is the *New Iridar* in danger? Are we in danger?" Jason asked.

"Let's move the ship back," Imanol suggested.

"What few eyes we have left are showing me everything is over," Telisa said. "The ship is gone. The guardians are out, but not shooting at anything."

"The ship left?"

"No, *New Iridar* says it's back in the building," Cilreth said.

"Everyone in," Telisa ordered. "I'll get patched up. You guys size up the damage to the Celarans. We need to find out if we're enemies now."

"Where did Vincent rescue you from?" Jason asked as he entered the ship.

"The Celarans gave me the look over," Siobhan said. "Though I saw only robots. Then they dropped me off in the forest with my stuff. My suit is damaged and out of power."

"By the Five," Telisa said. "I've screwed this up eight ways from extinction. We started this battle to try and get you back, but you were probably already released. Now we've made enemies of them."

"Maybe," Siobhan said. "The battle sphere is gone?"

Telisa did not answer. Jason could tell she was angry with herself.

Everyone rested for an hour and waited to see what would happen. Jason sat alone in his quarters and thought about his life.

Am I a core worlder or a frontiersman? Is this life better? Am I going to die too soon out here?

It seemed to Jason that one felt truly alive when danger threatened, yet that danger would eventually end his life. How could anyone balance that?

The core worlders had come to find that when they lived their virtual adventures in artificial worlds, their fun was muted by a lack of danger. Slowly new replacements to physical danger had been introduced, such as monetary penalties and bursts of pain used to provide meaning to failure in virtual reality. Some extremists actually suppressed or replaced their memories so that they did not know they were in a simulation until they died and woke up. A fraction of those maintained that their current life was also a simulation, and that they would awaken to a new reality when they died.

Jason saw now how those replacements paled compared to the incentives provided by real life on the frontier. An urgent message interrupted his thoughts.

"Interesting advance in the cargo bay," Cilreth announced. Jason left for the work area set up there.

"What?" Telisa asked on the channel.

"This is important. I think. Maybe. Look at these items. The all purpose laser, the unknown baton here, and this plain rod with all the complicated sub-sections of different materials... they are all the same mass. Just over three kilograms."

"That's all?" Imanol asked. "Some of us are hurt, you know."

"Interesting," Telisa said.

"It's important," Cilreth said, though she sounded like she might be convincing herself too. "I mean they are all *exactly* the same mass."

"That is important, it must be," Caden said.

"They were made from this," Siobhan asserted, picking up the plain rod. "These other two things started out like this thing."

"Ah, wow. Some kind of generic base material rod? But don't these two things require different materials?" asked Caden.

"They do. Kind of. Terrans would have used different materials. But these aliens—they like to be flexible, you know? They would have the same attitude about their materials. They have the variety they need here in this base rod. They would use materials that have a wide range of different uses. Like structural insulator, and a flexible conductor, vice-versa, each material selected for more than one possible function. Then through some advanced manufacturing process, maybe nanomachines, I don't know, they transformed it into what they needed."

"But we don't use different materials just for fun," Imanol said. "We do it because for any particular function, we choose the best material, well, tempered by its price anyway."

"These things have more than one function."

"But their components each do one thing... wouldn't they?"

"Imagine how much cheaper it would be to equip a new colony if you just manufactured these generic rods and could make a hundred different tools from the same thing?"

"It might even be programmable," Cilreth said. "Reconfigurable!"

"Amazing, if you're right," Caden said.

"The end result is inferior or we'd do this too," Imanol maintained.

"We prefer our way. They prefer theirs. They have different goals and ways of weighing success and failure," Telisa said. "You would have five tools Imanol. Each one may do its job very well. A Celaran only has to carry one tool instead of five. It might not be quite as good as each of your tools, but it was cheaper."

"And lighter! They are probably flyers, remember? One light multifunction rod would be important," Jason said.

Telisa nodded. "Exactly! See, it probably makes sense for them."

"That weight, or a multiple of it, is probably at an upper limit of what they would to carry with them on a flight," Caden said.

"That reminds me. I found out something about the laser," Telisa said. Telisa looked at the device, then she held it before her, level with the ground. Then she took her hand away. It floated in place.

"Whoa," Caden said.

"Wowsa, it hovers?" Cilreth said.

"As Jason says, perfect for a flyer. Or a glider," Telisa said. "They're all light. And this can hover. I bet the other one can, too."

"I'm working on verifying that these two different rods used the same material somewhere inside for two different reasons. Like something used as an insulator in one device that was used structurally in the other, something like that," Cilreth said.

"Okay, your theories sound good. I'd like to know what the other fully formed rod does," Imanol said. "That one's a laser. What's this?" Imanol pointed to the other tool.

"I can't figure it out yet," Cilreth said. "But the battery is smaller and it's much more mechanically complex."

"I'll have a crack at it," Telisa said.

"What's the plan, then? Just leave with what we have? Maybe take some parts from the houses?" Jason said.

"No, we have to neutralize the rest of the guard machines," Telisa said. "Or convince them to ignore us like they ignore Vincent."

"Then we would have access to all the toys," Caden said.

"I believe that's a spacecraft in there," Telisa said. "The thing that defeated the battle sphere. That's our objective. I think we could trade a Celaran spacecraft for Magnus."

"That's great! I agree. Surely Shiny would go for that," Siobhan said. "What's Magnus compared to an alien spaceship? I mean, to Shiny. Of course he's worth it to us."

"That's the plan. I hate to destroy more of the Celaran's stuff, but, first of all, I don't think any of them are here. Our need is great. Secondly, well, we already blew a bunch of stuff apart starting that fight with Shiny's battle sphere. As far as the Celarans are concerned, whether there are any of them or their AIs here, we are

Michael McCloskey

enemies. I'm skeptical they appreciate the distinction between the Vovokan battle sphere and us. If there is one. I mean, I decided to initiate that battle."

"Also, we have the attendants around us, also Vovokan," Imanol pointed out. "If an alien or an AI has watched us carefully, then they would probably conclude we are allies with the Vovokans. And we were at one time."

"We're going to set up an ambush," Telisa said. "The towers in our direction are destroyed. I'll go out onto the concrete or whatever it is, and when they come to get me, you'll be ready to snipe the security machines. Everyone, long range weapons. A mix of lasers and projectiles, please. Be ready in five minutes."

"No, that's not the way to go about it!" Siobhan said.
"Really?"

"They let me go. I was rudely examined, sure, but they let me go and even let me keep my equipment!"

"But we just had a major battle with them. They might not be so friendly now!"

"That was a Vovokan battle sphere. Lose the attendants and go in unarmed," Siobhan said.

"I don't think that's safe," Caden said.

"I'll take Vincent with me. He seems to get along fine with them."

Imanol and Telisa traded looks.

"When they first ran in there to get Telisa, I was shooting just after the sphere was destroyed," Imanol said. "Those are machines. They have to have noticed."

"We could test it," Cilreth said. "Send Vincent in with a simulacrum."

"Things this advanced would know the difference instantly," Telisa said. "Besides, do you have an android sitting around?"

"We need to make friends with them, not fight them," Siobhan said.

"I'd like to," Telisa said. "We were desperate because you had been captured."

"Okay, I want to go in with Vincent."

"Telisa can't send you in there on a crazy gamble. Your life is her responsibility," Caden sent to Jason. It looked to Jason like Telisa was not on the channel but Siobhan was.

"Shut up, she's thinking," Siobhan sent back.

"Normally I wouldn't allow it," Telisa said. "But it's so very important to be friends with these Celarans. So important maybe we should risk it. I'll go."

"You? We can't risk you."

Telisa snorted. "I'm a copy, remember? Besides, I'm in charge and I already decided."

"And if they vaporize you?" Cilreth asked.

"Then go back with some toys, prove yourselves valuable to Shiny, and tell him I died because Magnus wasn't here to help. Maybe he'll send both of us on the next expedition."

Telisa approached Vincent and motioned for him to follow. But the alien remained near Siobhan.

"He's been acting strange since saving me," Siobhan said. "And he sent some messages."

"Why didn't you say so?!" Imanol snapped.

"I am saying so. This is a war zone. I wanted to give Telisa time to recover."

"How has he been acting and what has he been saying?" Telisa asked.

"He hasn't left me since then," Siobhan said. "I've been afraid to try and avoid him because I owe him for that. He told me to walk. He told me to stop, just the nonverbal commands suite. He has my laser and I gave him permissions for it, though he can't shoot us."

"Uh oh. There may be some expectation on his part for payment," Caden said.

"I'd be happy to do what I could, but I don't know what he wants. And we're kind of broke now," Siobhan said.

That's true. We went from "you get whatever you want" to slaves of Shiny, Jason thought.

"There's nothing bad here, it's amazing we're finally starting to communicate with him!" Cilreth said.

"Especially given that as far as we know, communication is rare with Blackvines," Telisa said. "His use of commands is interesting. Think about it. A non-social creature might try commands first. It would treat us like machines to be controlled. It uses tools, computers, things like that. Anything external to itself would be thought of in the same light: things there to be used."

"Back to 'uh oh' then," Caden said. "We won't be able to have any meaningful exchange."

"Give him time. Question is, should Siobhan go out of her way to obey, so that he knows she can hear him, or should she not obey, to show that she's an independent entity?"

"Think on it. Come up with a plan. I'm going to check out that ship," Telisa said.

"Vincent won't come without me I think," Siobhan said.

"Then you're with me."

Telisa left her weapons and motioned for Siobhan to do the same. Caden and Imanol watched with obvious worry. Cilreth brought out two more rifles just in case. Jason realized most of them were injured from everything they had gone through.

At least we're alive. For the moment.

Telisa and Siobhan walked out of the forest and onto the hardtop. Siobhan and Vincent followed her out of the ship. Jason watched the feed from their eyes and stayed on the channel. He could tell Cilreth and Imanol were watching, too.

"I'm going out alone first."

"Come on, Telisa. You need Vincent."

"Does it really make sense for all of us to risk our lives together?" Telisa asked.

"No. It makes sense for me to go out with Vincent while you stay here."

"Stay here," Telisa ordered. She moved out to the remains of the nearest tower.

Telisa slowly walked out into the open. The *New Iridar* could see Celaran machines patrolling the area. Two of them peeled off to approach Telisa.

Vincent left Siobhan's position and made a beeline for Telisa.

"Okay, I think I've been accepted."

"Maybe," Imanol said. "Look behind you."

Telisa became aware of Vincent. The disc shape robots hovered nearby. One of them peeled off and left. The other stood by.

"Thank you, Vincent," she said.

"Forward."

Jason realized the nonverbal command came from Vincent. Jason's link had no voice profile to assign to Vincent's communications, so it sounded cold and artificial.

Telisa shrugged and walked forward.

"Okay, everyone. Looks like we got lucky. Myself, Siobhan, Caden and Vincent are heading in to look. Cilreth stays at the ship. The rest of you can look around but stay in these two buildings closest to the *New Iridar*. If you see an eight-armed robot then run for it. That's what their net trappers look like."

Wow. We're really just allowed in? Or are we being drawn out for the slaughter?

Jason decided he had been training with Imanol for too long. He headed over to the nearest building and prepared his smart rope.

"Let's see what we can see," Imanol said.

"What's up with that Vincent, anyway?" Jason said. "What's your analysis?"

"My *analysis*? My analysis is that that big black weed is going to screw us over just like Shiny did," Imanol said.

"Bet on it?" Jason said.

"What could we possibly bet?" Imanol said.

Jason checked back with Telisa's team. They had made it to the top of the spacecraft hangar building.

"It's not letting us through," Telisa said.

"I guess we're friends, but not close friends," Siobhan summarized.

"We're on probation since we trashed part of the complex," Cilreth said from the ship.

"Then what did Vincent do?"

"Good question."

Chapter 18

Caden stood with Telisa and Siobhan atop the Celaran building. Vincent scuttled about nearby. Caden was still riding high on his relief that Siobhan had returned. He still keenly felt the precarious nature of their lives. She might have never come back.

Telisa must think of Magnus a lot, he thought. *She's patient, though. She had no choice.*

"This is the building," Telisa said.

Caden saw Vincent hovering around a hatchway leading into the building.

"Vincent knows something interesting is in there, too," Caden noted.

Siobhan went over and tried to open the door flaps again. They refused to budge.

"No go," she said.

"Is this punishment for the attack? Or just... they've become more cautious?" Caden wondered aloud.

"There's a puzzle here," Telisa said. "Vincent could go into the compound at will, but could not get through any of the doors. We've always been allowed through the doors, until now."

"Not true," Imanol said to the group channel. He transmitted to them from the top of an adjacent building. "I'm free to enter this area."

"Then investigate," Telisa sent back.

"Okay. Certain areas are restricted," Caden said. "And is it really surprising? They won't let us in the building with the spacecraft."

"They. They who?" Siobhan said.

"Probably an AI," Caden said. "Or computers, robots, whatever."

"Okay. Investigate what you can. Collect what you can. Don't try to force anything. We'll show 'them' we're just curious," Telisa said.

Telisa stayed with Caden and Siobhan as they went from building to building, checking their access and snooping around. The robots were always nearby, but they did not encounter any of the net throwers and nothing interfered with their investigation. Most of the structures housed complex factories of staggering complexity. Knowing what they did about the Celarans and their love of multifunction systems, it seemed likely the complex could produce anything needed for a large colony.

Hours later, each of them had as many artifacts as they could carry. Unfortunately most of them were alike. Either batons like the ones they had already, or what they thought were spare parts for the robots or hexagonal wall blocks as were used in the houses. The team was about to head back to the *New Iridar* for the day when their links got a message.

"We've made a breakthrough," Cilreth transmitted from back near the ship. "Imanol and Jason found more of those black cloth items. A lot more. We've been looking them over."

"We'll be there in just a few minutes," Telisa said eagerly. "What's the gist of it?" Telisa headed back for the smart ropes they used to scale the building.

"I figured them out. I know what these are and I know more about the Celarans."

Telisa hurried over to the edge of the building and started down. Everyone followed, even Vincent. Caden shared Telisa's urgency to learn about the Celarans. They double timed it down to the flat surface of the field and across to the border.

Two robots worked to repair the fence, one from each side. They avoided the machines and walked through the center. Caden spotted Cilreth in their small camp set up just outside the old compound net. Everyone gathered around Cilreth in the tiny encampment. She had the black things arrayed around her on top of Vovokan equipment containers.

"So what are these things?" Telisa asked.

"Here's the key: we found them in four different sizes. There are a very large number in this biggest size. The other three sizes, well, there's a lot less of those."

"Clothes?"

"Well, you know the Celarans. They're more like, clothes, link, medical kit, chameleon suit, battery, fly booster and Cthulhu knows what else. It's decked out eight ways from extinction."

Telisa picked one of the suits up and tried to make heads or tails of it.

"Clothes? So this is the biggest clue we're going to get as to what they look like," Siobhan said.

Caden took a suit and started to look it over too. "Uhhh," he said helplessly. "This is like trying to figure out women's clothing before I got old enough to want to learn how to take it all off."

"I cracked that one too," Cilreth said. She brought up a pointer and passed it out to their links. Caden accessed it and brought up picture of a creature wearing the outfit in his PV.

"The glider snakes are the Celarans!" Jason said.

"Well, probably no, they're all too small. The most common size fits one about two and a half meters long."

"But if the shoe fits... sorry. You know what I mean."

Caden looked at the outfit and Cilreth's concept rendering. There was no question it was for a creature just like the glider snakes. The entire thing was symmetrical along two axes, just like the glider snakes. The black part covered the top, complete with a webwork of miniature equipment embedded inside. The straps or bands came around to secure it, and they were spaced perfectly to allow the glowing chevrons on the underside to be seen.

Probably that's how they speak, Caden thought again. *Those light patterns. Though at this level they must have links, inside or in those suits.*

The garment was widest in the middle, and connected from one end to the other with a hole in the center where they glider snakes were thickest.

"Any idea about the hole? They don't have anything there, do they?" Caden asked.

"Light sensors," Cilreth said. "They also have some more on each end, around the fingers."

"Too weird. Creepy," Siobhan said.

"Two hands, six fingers," Telisa said. "It makes sense. I suspect base six math. There were 36 towers around the third site. And they seem partial to hexagons, that may be related."

"But with a hand on each end like that, they can't move and use their hands at the same time," Imanol said.

"Every race has its advantages and limitations. I think these guys can eat and breathe at the same time, for instance," Telisa said.

"Yeah, eat and... it never comes out," Jason said.

"We don't know that," Telisa said. "Shiny regurgitates his old meals. Eventually. So they could do that, too. But I think this tree sap may be so pure, and they may have evolved to eat only that one thing, so maybe their bodies know how to use every bit of it."

"But a metabolism—" Cilreth said.

"Waste gases?" Siobhan said.

"Basic hollow tube structure, seems like an almost universal design. Food goes in and comes out. Though here both ends look the same... which end is which?" Imanol said.

"No idea just yet," Telisa said. "Let's move on. Why are these Celarans all so stunted? Maybe some environmental disaster on the new planet they did not anticipate?"

"Or maybe these are a dumber larval form," Imanol said.

"A possibility," Siobhan said. "Another one is that those things are to the Celarans like monkeys or primates are to us. They just happen to be the most similar life form from the same planet, but they fall short of intelligence."

"Ah. Good theory. Imagine the confusion if an alien landed on our planet and found primates in the jungle outside an abandoned human city!" Telisa said.

"They could still be similar to dogs and cats or something," Jason said. "We don't usually have primate pets but they might enjoy domestic creatures very similar to themselves."

"They could be testing the terraform," Caden said. "If Celarans are closely related to those things, they could see if the planet is safe by observing how those things fare here. Maybe they haven't arrived yet, or something went wrong and they're not coming."

Telisa brightened. "Now we're producing some great ideas."

"But the robots could tell if it's safe here," Imanol said.

"To some degree. This is a more robust way to check the chemical and biological safety?"

"They would be pretty mean to send their equivalent of primates to live here and just see if they live or die," Siobhan said.

"Maybe yes. Maybe it's not wrong by their mores to do such a thing. Or maybe they were almost certain it's safe before the creatures were populated here," Telisa said.

"But they never showed up. So maybe they *were* wrong," Imanol said.

"Well we still have no real live Celarans. But we do have a lot of toys to play with," Cilreth said brightly.

Michael McCloskey

Chapter 19

Cilreth went to visit Telisa in her tiny quarters on the *New Iridar*. She found Telisa brooding.

And I think I know what about, Cilreth thought. They had been collecting samples of Celaran technology from all accessible areas of the base for three days. The cargo hold was full of large numbers of hovering tech batons, Celaran clothing, and spare parts. They had not found any quiescent robots to steal, nor had they dared to capture any.

"How are we going to get that Celaran ship out of there?" Cilreth asked. "I don't know the first thing about it. My brain is already full of Terran and Vovokan stuff. It pains me to think about learning Celaran next."

Said like a true old timer.

"I'm not sure that we're going to get it out of there," Telisa said. "I suspected you might feel that way, so I've asked Siobhan and Caden to learn everything they can about the Celaran cybernetics."

"She has a more technical background," Cilreth said.

"And he's highly intelligent and competitive. It can't hurt to challenge him."

"Yes. I agree," Cilreth said. "I'm surprised to hear you say we might not be taking it."

"It's not our ship to take."

"Well, it might be if the Celaran civilization is dead," Cilreth said. "And we already shot the place up..."

"How secure is this ship now that we got rid of that watchdog?" Telisa asked, dodging the topic.

"I imagine the attendants are impossible to make safe," Cilreth said. "My guess is, Shiny has ways to take control of them I can't do anything about, since I'm not allowed into those systems. But at least they almost certainly don't have the power to make tachyonic transmissions."

Should I have said that with so much confidence? On the other side of the light barrier, faster transmissions actually take less power, not more... if the Vovokans can intercept insanely fast messages...

"I thought we had complete control of them."

"Oh they seem to take our orders, all right. But we don't have core access. They just do what we say... I think they will do what Shiny says over us. The *New Iridar* is a brighter story, though. I have direct access to the core system. I learned a lot on the *Clacker*..."

And I wish my double was here, because she was even better at this than I am.

"Do you think he's tracking us? Do you think he could remotely recall the ship? Does he know if we're alive or dead? Is he listening to our every word?"

Cilreth sighed.

"Well. The ship will send a message before it dies if it can. I could turn that off, but I figured, if we die, no harm in letting him know the particulars. This far out, I don't think he can track us using the normal setup. He might have attached an isolated system that transmits tachyons, then blinded our sensors to it. But where would the power come from?"

"Where, indeed," Telisa said in that way that meant she wanted Cilreth to check it out.

"I think I have genuine control of the ship. But I'm not the equivalent of a Vovokan hacker. Let's face it, there have to be advanced methods they use to hijack systems, and how can I really be aware of those?"

Telisa's face showed a pained look.

I just can't give her the answers she wants.

"I'm sorry, Telisa, but this is an alien ship, and they're so advanced—"

"I get it. That's okay. I prefer you honest, even if it makes me want to shoot myself."

"Then let me say a human ship might not be much better. Shiny has studied human computer systems and I'm sure he knows how to compromise those, too. Given his vast computing power, amazing tech, and a Trilisk AI to listen to his prayers, it's probably child's play to him."

Telisa did not say anything.

She has to be thinking about getting Magnus back!

"I think we could trade the Celaran ship for Magnus," Cilreth said. "It's got to be a juicy find. Who knows what that ship is capable of?"

Telisa nodded. "Maybe. We don't even have access to it at the moment. We'll give Shiny everything else—the clothes and the tools and the robots. We can even take one of the houses apart for its components before we leave."

"So what now? We just go back to Earth?"

Telisa did not answer immediately. After long seconds she shook her head.

"We got rid of that damn watchdog of his. I don't want to go back yet just to have another one put back into the cargo hold. I want to talk to real Celarans. If we can make friends with them, they could help us so much."

"We have no idea what they're like," Cilreth said. "They might be ornery."

"Well at least we know they don't bite," Telisa smiled.

Cilreth raised an eyebrow.

"I'm going to risk it," Telisa continued. "We keep the ship as our ace in the hole. Find the Celarans without our watchdog and make a deal with them. Maybe they can help us with our Shiny problem."

"Last time we—"

"'Maybe' I said. Aliens are by definition different from each other. The Celarans won't be Trilisks and they won't be Vovokans. They might be friendly. We're due to find some friendly aliens, don't you think?"

"Maybe the nice ones don't make it. They get steamrolled by the aggressive dominant races," Cilreth said.

"I want to find out."

"Where are we going to find these Celarans?"

"The next planet on the route," Telisa said. "These are all supposed to be Celaran sites. And supposedly we know the homeworld, too."

"Okay, I'm in. Gotta convince the others, though."

Telisa smiled sadly. "Where else do they have to go?"

11219986R00119